DOWN HOME
AND DEADLY

This Large Print Book carries the
Seal of Approval of N.A.V.H.

ALIBIS IN ARKANSAS, BOOK 3

DOWN HOME AND DEADLY

A SLEUTHING SISTERS MYSTERY

CHRISTINE LYNXWILER, JAN REYNOLDS, AND SANDY GASKIN

THORNDIKE PRESS

A part of Gale, Cengage Learning

GALE
CENGAGE Learning™

Detroit • New York • San Francisco • New Haven, Conn • Waterville, Maine • London

GALE
CENGAGE Learning™

Thorndike Press, a part of Gale, Cengage Learning.

ALL RIGHTS RESERVED

This book is a work of fiction. Names, characters, places, and incidents are either products of the author's imagination or are used fictitiously, as explained in the author's note. Any similarity to actual people, organizations, and/or events is purely coincidental.

Thorndike Press® Large Print Christian Mystery.
The text of this Large Print edition is unabridged.
Other aspects of the book may vary from the original edition.
Set in 16 pt. Plantin.
Printed on permanent paper.

LIBRARY OF CONGRESS CATALOGING-IN-PUBLICATION DATA

Lynxwiler, Christine.
 Down home and deadly : a sleuthing sisters mystery / by Christine Lynxwiler, Jan Reynolds, Sandy Gaskin.
  p. cm. — (Alibis in Arkansas ; bk. 3)
 "Thorndike Press large print Christian mystery."
 ISBN-13: 978-1-4104-2026-8 (hardcover : alk. paper)
 ISBN-10: 1-4104-2026-4 (hardcover : alk. paper)
 1. Sisters—Fiction. 2. Murder—Investigation—Fiction.
 3. Diners (Restaurants)—Fiction. 4. Arkansas—Fiction. 5. Large type books. I. Reynolds, Jan (Jan Pearle) II. Gaskin, Sandy.
 III. Title.
 PS3612.Y554D69 2009
 813'.6—dc22   2009029591

Published in 2009 by arrangement with Barbour Publishing, Inc.

Printed in the United States of America
1 2 3 4 5 6 7 13 12 11 10 09

DEDICATION

To our brothers and sisters at Ward St. Church of Christ, Southwest Church of Christ, and Beedeville Church of Christ for your incredible love and support. May God continue to richly bless you as you work for him.

1

If you lay down with the dogs,
you'll come up with fleas.

"Don't forget to call the groomer to see what time you should pick up Fluffy," Lisa yelled over her shoulder as she headed toward the sauna.

I slumped into my chair and reached for the phone book. Nepotism was alive and well in America, and my so-called career was a train wreck.

Actually, train wreck was probably a little too dramatic. More like an economy car, really. With a dead battery. And me trudging along behind, pushing uphill.

I waved my hand in front of my face, trying to disperse the cloying scent of Lisa's expensive perfume. How did I get here? A year ago I was a valued employee, on the fast track to buying my boss's health club for a good price, with the added bonus of owner financing. Until Bob asked me to show his rich daughter a little about running the club to help her get her confidence back after her recent separation from her husband.

If Lisa had a confidence problem, she covered it well with a large mask of egotism. Ever since she showed up, I'd been edging closer and closer to becoming an indentured servant. I still had all my old tasks. (Lisa couldn't figure out how to actually *run* the club, only how to use the equipment.) But in addition, I was her daytime maid.

"How low can I go?" I complained to the empty office and picked up the phone, a prayer for patience running through my mind as I flipped through the business card index for the groomer's number.

Wait until Carly heard this one. At the thought of my sister's reaction, my gaze went automatically to the family picture I kept on my desk. Or rather to the place it used to be. "I don't believe it." My picture had been replaced by one of Lisa cuddling her pampered pooch.

I slammed the phone down. "That *so* does it."

Without stopping to analyze, I grabbed an empty plastic bag from Lisa's expensive takeout lunch and filled it with my personal things. The things I could find.

I yanked open the top drawer of the desk. There was my family picture. At least it didn't get thrown out with the garbage. Or stuck in the pool supply closet, like all my paintings from the office wall did when I took a Branson trip awhile back. "She can put up all the modern art she wants now," I muttered as I cleaned out the drawer.

Satisfied I had everything I couldn't live without, I snatched up my keys. "I'm outta here."

I stomped down the hall, pushed open the front door, and crashed into Bob.

"Jenna?" He shifted the box he was carrying to effectively block my exit. "What are you doing?"

I took a reluctant step back into the building. "Leaving."

"When will you be back?"

When your daughter figures out she isn't the queen of the universe. "When you're ready to sign on the dotted line and make me the owner." Same thing.

His face reddened. "Ah, Jenna. I was about ready to do that, actually. But something's come up and I'm a little short on cash. So even if I did sell it to you now, I couldn't owner finance. My accountant . . ."

I hadn't been impressed the first time Bob

told me what excuse he and his accountant had cooked up for not selling me the place, and I sure didn't plan to stay around and listen to it again. I put my hand on the box to move it out of my way.

"Wait!" Bob quickly opened the box and pulled something from it. He gave me his most suave smile and dropped the box at his feet. He held up a blue T-shirt. White lettering across the front commanded, "Get in the Swim with Jenna Stafford."

I frowned. He hoped to win me over with the very T-shirts I'd protested? Capitalizing on my Olympic glory (or lack thereof, in my opinion, considering I lost) had been the thing I disliked most about this job. A necessary evil. But definitely not a persuasion point for staying.

His smile stretched wider. "I know how you always hated the pink ones, so I got them in blue."

I sighed. "We both know who asked for them in blue." Demanded was more like it. "And speaking of her . . ." I moved the T-shirt out of my way like a bull charging a red cloth and brushed past him. "You'd better call the groomer to see what time you should pick up Fluffy." The door closed behind me.

Thankfully he didn't follow me.

Something about standing in front of the familiar building with my belongings in a plastic bag made my insides quiver. After months of giving notice then giving in to Bob's pleading to stay, I'd finally done it. I'd quit. I took a deep breath of fresh September air and exhaled slowly. Would I be sorry? Eventually, maybe, but not today.

My cell rang before I got to my vehicle. I glanced at the caller ID. Bob. Probably couldn't find the groomer's number. I ignored the call and stowed my stuff in the front seat of the SUV. Before I could turn the key, Sister Sledge belted out, "We Are Family."

I jumped. Since my old phone was at the bottom of Table Rock Lake, I'd been forced to get a new one. And I still hadn't gotten used to the personalized ringtones my nephew Zac had set up for me. What was it with teenagers and technology? And why did my youthful thirty suddenly seem so old?

At least I had sense enough to know that ringtone was my sister, Carly. Just what I needed — a sympathetic ear.

I flipped the phone open.

She started to talk so fast I couldn't understand a single word.

"Carly. Slow down."

"The. Grand. Opening. Of. Down Home. Diner. It's two weeks from Friday. That's sixteen days." She enunciated her words as if English was my second language. Or third.

Even though buying and refurbishing the Lake View Diner had been Carly's dream, the realization of that dream was proving a wee bit stressful. "I know that. Remember, I made sure I wasn't on the schedule at the athletic club that day so that I could help you?" I started the engine. "Not that it matters now."

"What do you mean, it doesn't matter now?" The frantic tone was back. "It matters to me. I need your help!"

"You've got it. As much as you need." I resisted the urge to peel out of the parking lot as I raged about the injustices I'd endured. She sympathized until finally my white-knuckle grip on the steering wheel relaxed. When I was almost home, I half-laughed. "Sorry for ranting so long. But that's it. I'm not working there anymore."

"When I called, I was going to ask you to see if Bob could let you have a few days off. But now, with you quitting, well, this is just perfect." I guess she heard herself, because she hastily added, "Heaven knows I've been so irritated at Bob since he brought Lisa in and made you a flunky."

"Thanks for clearing up any remaining delusions I might have had about my job."

"Hey, that's what sisters are for." Carly paused. "You okay with this?"

"Sure. I will be." I slowed at my street and turned on the blinker then glanced in the rearview mirror. Not a car in sight. So at least my boss hadn't followed me home. "And I really don't want to talk to Bob for a few days, anyway." With any other job, I'd have felt bad about not giving notice, but I *had* been giving notice ever since Lisa came. Bob just hadn't been listening.

"Great. How fast can you get over here?"

"Who put that table with a checker set on it out on the porch?" Alice asked, her graying brows drawn together.

Carly looked up from a booth where she'd spent the morning interviewing wait staff and cooks. "I did."

Alice pursed her lips and nodded.

Carly gave me a look that said, "Can you handle this, please?" and turned back to Vini, a young Albanian who'd done a great job working at the health club for several months. Until Lisa fired him a couple of days ago out of the blue. I'd asked Carly to interview him, so I owed her.

I put my hand on Alice's arm. "You've been working hard. I made some tea awhile ago. Want some?"

Alice nodded. "That sounds good."

I picked up my cell phone off the counter and slid it into my pocket as I pushed open the double doors. Something about the new phone made it hard to keep up with. I didn't even remember putting it there.

Alice followed me into the kitchen. "Don't get me wrong. I'm thrilled your sister wanted to buy our diner, but she sure has some strange ideas."

"Change is never easy." I smiled at my reflection in the stainless steel side-by-side refrigerator. I'd been moonlighting incognito for about a year as local advice columnist Dear Pru. Now I was starting to sound like her in my everyday conversations. "You loved the diner just like it was." I handed her a glass of ice.

She gave me a sharp look.

"I mean, everyone did. Love it," I stammered. So much for being wise. "But it's normal for Carly to want to do some things to make it her own."

"Carly might do well to remember what your mama always says."

I poured tea into her glass. "What's that?" Unlike me, our mama is a fount of wisdom.

Hard to know which thing Alice was referring to.

"If it ain't broke, don't fix it." She took a big chug of her tea.

I was pretty sure my mama had never said the word *ain't* in her life, but I had heard her echo that general sentiment before. "Oh. Yeah."

Harvey pushed open the doors. "You know why she's got that table out on the porch?"

Alice shook her head, and I didn't breathe. The table on the porch was just a tiny piece of the bigger picture my sister had in mind. But telling Alice and Harvey had been the fly in the ointment from the beginning. And I wasn't about to take on the task.

Harvey grunted. "She's got some fool idea about people playing dominoes and checkers out there."

Alice gasped. "Did you tell her that this is a diner? The whole idea is to get people to eat and then leave so more people can eat."

Harvey grabbed a hammer from the closet and headed back out. "I told her," he called over his shoulder. "But beneath that soft drawl, she's got a mind of her own."

Did I detect a bit of admiration in his voice? Harvey and Alice had been our parents' friends for so long, that I could definitely understand why it was hard for them to see Carl and Elizabeth's little girls trying to make over the diner they'd poured their hearts and souls into all these years.

"Checkers and dominoes," Alice scoffed under her breath as she finished off her tea. "Might as well put rocking chairs out there, too."

I don't play poker. And it's a good thing. Because my poker face wouldn't fool anyone.

Alice looked at me, and her eyes widened in disbelief. "You don't mean it?"

I nodded. Why hadn't Carly just come clean with them about her big plans? She'd convinced herself — and me — that they'd take it easier in small bites. I wasn't so sure.

Alice huffed out. I savored the peacefulness of the quiet kitchen and considered calling Alex to invite him to come help us paint tonight. We needed all the hands we could get. And it'd definitely be more fun with him here. That was a no-brainer. I pulled my phone from my pocket and hit the button that redials the last number dialed.

"Hey, babe."

I frowned. That didn't sound like my fiancé, but I thought sure he was the last one I called. "Alex?"

"I'm sorry. I believe you have the wrong number."

I held the phone out and looked at the screen. It read — "Connected to Me." What did that even mean? I groaned inwardly. "Sorry. My bad."

I pushed the END button just as the double doors opened again and Debbie walked in with a roll of wallpaper in her hand. The waitress had been so thrilled to stay on at the diner that she'd offered to help out with the remodeling. Carly had accepted and gladly agreed to pay her. Even though I had two strikes against me with her — one, that she'd always liked Alex, and two, that she was Lisa's best friend — she'd been nothing but friendly to me.

When she saw me, her eyes widened and she stopped. "Is that my phone?"

I smiled. "No, this is my new —" My smile faded as I remembered the wrong number. I held up the phone. "Does your phone look like this?"

"Yes."

I ducked my head. "I'm sorry. So does mine. Exactly. I haven't had mine long enough to tell it from someone else's, I guess." I held it out to her.

She snatched the phone out of my hand. "Did you use it?"

I stared at her. Talk about overreacting. Even if her cell phone minutes were limited, I'd only had the phone for a minute. "I hit the last call dialed, thinking I'd call Alex, but obviously it wasn't him."

She didn't answer, just mashed a couple of buttons on the phone and stared at the screen. "Did you talk to someone?"

I'd been interrogated by police that weren't this stern. "Just a guy who said I had the wrong number. I'm sorry I got confused."

Her smile looked a little forced, but at least it was a smile. She pushed a strand of her bleached-blond hair behind her ear. "No worries. That happens. I just got mine too, yesterday."

"And wouldn't you know I'd steal it today? We need to get one of those label makers. Remember those? When I was about ten, Mama got one to label things at the cabins, and I labeled the whole house. Even the furniture."

Her smile relaxed. "I do remember those. One summer I went to camp with 'Debbie' in raised white letters on bright blue tape stuck on everything I owned."

Raised voices in the dining room interrupted our soft laughter.

"Do they know yet?" Debbie whispered.

I shrugged. "It sounds like maybe they do now."

With trepidation, I walked over to the door and peeked out. Vini was gone, and Carly stood facing Harvey and Alice, who had their backs to me.

Carly saw me and motioned me to her. "Jenna, come tell them that you think the new name is great."

I looked over my shoulder at Debbie, who shooed me out. "I'll just be in here hanging wallpaper and minding my own business."

"Chicken," I muttered. I walked over to the tense trio. "You have to admit that 'Down Home Diner' has a ring to it."

"What does 'down home' mean, anyway?" Alice asked, her nose crinkling as if a skunk had suddenly crawled up under the diner and died.

"You know what 'down home' means," Harvey insisted. "Country and common." He waved his hand to the porch. "That's why that table's out there, obviously. Checkers and dominoes are 'down home.' "

She narrowed her eyes at her husband. "Whose side are you on?"

"You know I'm on your side. I always have been. I was just answering your question."

Alice took a couple of steps backward, and Harvey pulled a chair out for her to sit on.

Seated, she looked up at Carly, her eyes swimming with tears. "We should have put in the contract that you couldn't do that." She grabbed a paper napkin from the table in front of her and wiped her nose. She motioned toward the small delicately lettered sign Carly had just finished and placed on the pie counter. "It's crazy enough to be giving police officers in uniform a free piece of pie. But I'd never have thought of anyone changing the name of the diner."

Harvey ran his finger around the collar of his checked shirt. "Actually, remember when Mom and Pop first turned the diner over to us? You wanted to rename it Alice's Restaurant. But Mom had a fit."

For a second, Alice's face opened as if she were remembering a younger her — full of plans and hopes. But then she pinched her lips together and shrugged. "And rightly so. I was a silly kid who didn't know what was what."

I glanced at Carly, wondering how she'd handle the inference. But her Southern graciousness won out.

"I'm sorry I hurt your feelings, Alice," she said softly. "But this is a fresh start for me. And the Down Home Diner is what I need."

My sister, the quintessential steel magnolia.

Alice slumped. "Oh, it's okay. You bought it. You should be able to call it whatever you want. I'm just an old fool."

Harvey sat down beside her and patted her hand. "This is a fresh start for us, too, Allie. Heaven knows we need one. And I think it'll be easier for us to let go of the Down Home Diner than the Lake View Diner."

She nodded. "You might be right."

In unspoken agreement, we left them to their own conversation and walked out onto the front porch.

Carly sat down at the small table that had started all of this and motioned me to sit across from her. She mussed her dark curls with her hand in a mannerism I recognized meant she had something on her mind.

"What's up?" I asked.

She picked up a red checker and tapped it against the table absently. "Nothing really. Not yet, anyway."

"What does that mean? Is it about the diner? Or Elliott?" Ever since I'd gotten engaged a few weeks ago, I'd been wondering about Carly and Elliott. Apparently that old adage about those in love wanting everyone to be in love was true.

"You know Elliott and I are getting pretty serious."

I propped my elbows on the table and leaned toward her. "Yes?"

She turned the checker up on its edge and rolled it from one hand to another across the wooden surface.

"Carly! What's going on?" Patience wasn't my strong point. And she knew it.

"I'm thinking about trying to find Travis," she said in a rush.

"Why?" I blurted out. Her ex-husband, Travis, had divorced her when she was pregnant with the twins and Zac was six. He'd run off with an emaciated model and eventually skipped the country to Mexico. We assumed he left the country to keep from paying child support. I'd loved my brother-in-law once, back before he betrayed our whole family and broke my sister's heart. But going searching for him made about as much sense to me as trying to bring back a bad migraine once it was gone.

She carefully placed the checker back in its original place on the board and looked up at me. "For closure for the kids. And for me, too, really. If we get married, Elliott would like to adopt them, and I'd like that, too. Even though I feel sure we could get it approved on grounds of abandonment, I'd rather have Travis's permission."

I shook my head. "My gut is saying that finding Travis is a terrible idea, Carly. In this case, I can't think of any better advice than to let sleeping dogs lie." Or in Travis's case, let lying dogs sleep, but I didn't say that out loud. "What does Elliott think?"

She bit her lower lip and pushed her curls back from her face. "He agrees with you."

I didn't know what to say. Nobody likes to feel ganged up on. "So how's the hiring process going?"

She grimaced to let me know she knew what I was doing, but picked up the new subject. "Pretty good. I kept Arnie to wash dishes but hired a new guy, too. Same with the cook. Of course, most of the new staff isn't starting until after the grand opening, since Harvey and Alice are going to help out with that. Hard to believe those two were doing half the cooking and dishwashing themselves."

I idly moved a black checker. "They don't have kids," I reminded her. "The twins and Zac would be disappointed if you turned into a workaholic."

She laughed and slid a red checker forward one space. "The twins might be. But now that he's a senior, Zac thinks he doesn't need his mama anymore."

"Is he going to work here after school?" I

moved another checker.

She nodded as she responded with a move of her own. "I'll have some part-time hours for him. Most of the waitresses stayed on, though. And I hired Vini as a waiter."

I smiled. "Oh, good. He always impressed me with his work ethic at the gym. He's punctual and never goofs off."

"I hired him already. You can stop the streaming reference message."

"Did you call Lisa about him?" I asked as I considered my next move.

"Didn't think I needed to with you here," Carly said, edging her checker close to being able to jump mine. "Especially since he was honest about her firing him."

I frowned and pushed my black playing piece out of harm's way. "Did he say what reason she gave?"

Carly shook her head and countered with another move. "Just said she fired him for no good reason."

"Sounds like her." With Lisa on my mind, I shoved my checker hard without really thinking.

Carly reached across, jumped over two of my checkers, and scooped them up.

"Wait a minute!" I protested. "I wasn't paying attention."

"When you play on my porch, you should

always pay attention," she said facetiously. "Welcome to the Down Home Diner."

"Jenna."

I spun around with the dishcloth still in my hand.

Carly, her dark hair curling around her sweaty face, beamed at me from the kitchen window. "Can you snag the garbage when you're done?"

"Sure. Why not?" I wiped the crumbs from the counter into my hand and waggled my fingers over the trash can. Across the room, Harvey patiently showed Vini how to clean the salad bar at the close of the day. I pushed the kitchen door open with my shoulder. "Carly, if success can be measured by garbage, I'd say your grand opening was a resounding triumph."

Carly looked up from stirring a large pot of tomorrow's soup of the day she already had simmering over the burner. "You think so?"

I washed my hands at the stainless steel double sink.

"She's right." Alice reached across Carly and salted the soup. "Harvey took it out not twenty minutes ago."

Carly put her hand on Alice's. "I already salted it."

"I know you did, honey, but just not enough for bean soup. Beans absorb salt like little sponges." Hearty shakes of salt punctuated each word.

Carly tossed me a pleading look over her shoulder. That old saying about too many cooks spoiling the broth was definitely proving true during this transition period of old diner owner to new.

I gathered the handles of the black plastic bag and cleared my throat. "Alice, thanks to that last rush of police officers we had an hour ago, most of the pie is gone. But there are a few pieces left in each pan. What do you do with those?"

Alice glanced out at the pie counter. "Wrap up individual servings and sell them at breakfast. I'll take care of them." She headed toward the door. "I still don't know about this idea of giving away pie," she said over her shoulder.

When the door swung shut behind the older woman, Carly sighed. "Thanks for rescuing me." She opened a drawer and dropped the saltshaker into it. "Why did I think it would be a good idea to accept their offer to help me out for a while?"

"It was a good idea. Besides, in a few weeks this place will be all yours." I lifted the plastic bags, one in each hand, and slipped out the back door. The door slammed loudly behind me. I stepped off the back porch into the orange glow of the quiet alley. Whoever invented guard lights deserves a Nobel Prize. Or at least a free piece of pie.

I duckwalked to the Dumpster, balancing my burdens. "One, two, three, heave." I threw one garbage bag into the green Dumpster, then let go of the other one. It went flying over the trash bin and landed with a thud. A small noise made me jump.

"Shifting trash," I whispered and tiptoed around to retrieve the bag.

I squinted at the darker area behind the Dumpster then put my hand out to touch the warm hood of a small sports car I hadn't even seen. Why would it be parked here, completely hidden by the huge double Dumpster? The owner took the thing about not wanting to risk having anyone hit his door in the parking lot to a whole new level. I stretched to get the trash bag off the roof and froze.

This car had more than a dent in the door. The driver window was broken out. I snagged the handle of the bag but stopped again. A man I didn't recognize was slumped sideways in the front seat.

"Sir?" My voice was as jagged as the

window I was looking through.

He didn't respond. Being careful to avoid the broken glass, I reached in and touched his left shoulder. Still no response. I touched his neck for a pulse.

No pulse. My hand brushed sticky wetness at the same time I saw the dark stain on his shirt, and I knew I was in a deserted alley with a dead body.

Something rustled behind me. I started to turn, but the world exploded. Darkness rushed to meet me.

2

Dead as a doornail

"Oww . . ." I'm not sure if the sound of groaning woke me or if the pain woke me and then I groaned. Either way, I opened my eyes and reached toward the black thing in front of me. At least that's what my brain said for me to do. My arms, apparently trapped under my body too long, weren't getting the signal. I rolled over and ignored the pins and needles as I shifted to sitting. Nausea hit in waves.

My head throbbed. "Oww . . ." At least now that I was upright, I could identify the black thing as a tire. I rubbed my fat-feeling fingers over my stinging cheek, and pieces of gravel clinked to the ground. Why had I been facedown in the gravel next to a car? As soon as the question flitted through my pounding brain, I knew the answer.

I was in the alley behind the diner.

And there was a dead man in the car beside me.

But the dead man hadn't knocked me out. I turned my head fractionally, wincing with every muscle shift. No captor stood nearby waiting for me to wake. I appeared to be alone, thankfully.

How long had I been out here? I squinted through the dim alley past the Dumpster. The back door of the diner looked miles away. The feeling was coming back in my fingers, and I eased myself up onto wobbly legs and gritted my teeth. "You can do it," I whispered and limped toward the distant porch light.

Finally, my hand closed around the doorknob and turned. I pulled the door open. Debbie, in an apron, didn't look up from where she rapidly loaded the dishwasher. Vini stood at the sink with his back to me.

I stumbled into the room feeling as if I'd stumbled into a Twilight Zone episode. Why hadn't someone come looking for me? Alice bustled into the kitchen holding a broom with one hand and a dustpan in the other.

As much out of a need to assure myself that I wasn't invisible to my coworkers as anything else, I opened my mouth to speak. Before I could, the kitchen door swung again, and Carly rushed in, her gaze immediately falling on me. "There you are. Were you cleaning the bathrooms?" She narrowed her eyes. "Why is there dirt on your face? What's wrong? Are you okay?" Her voice rose with each question, and silence filled the room as everyone stopped what they were doing and turned to look at us.

"Dead man."

"What?" Carly peered at me, confusion knitting her brows together.

I tried again. "A man was shot out behind the Dumpster. He's dead."

I heard gasps from every corner. "Are you sure he is dead?" Vini asked weakly.

"Yes," I gasped out. "I think the killer is still out there. Somebody knocked me out." My knees gave way, and they all rushed toward me.

Carly grabbed me around the waist, and Debbie shoved a chair under me. "Call 911," she barked to Vini, whose normally swarthy complexion looked pale and sallow.

"I'll do it." Alice yanked up the cordless phone. "Harvey," she yelled as she punched in the numbers.

"It hasn't been ten minutes since the last police officer left. Too bad they didn't stay a little longer." Debbie grabbed a bag of frozen peas from the huge side-by-side

31

freezer, wrapped a towel around it, and carefully placed it against the back of my head. "Did you see anyone else parked out there? On the edge of the parking lot? Or in the alley?"

Before I could answer, Harvey came running in. "What's wrong?"

Alice shushed him as the 911 operator apparently answered.

He glanced over at me and did a double take. "What happened?" he whispered as Alice rattled off who she was and where she was.

"There's a dead man in the alley," Alice said bluntly into the receiver.

Harvey spun around toward her. "A what?"

"A dead man," she mouthed and waved him away. "He's been shot. And Jenna Stafford found the body. Yes. Jenna Stafford. She's been hurt. Someone knocked her out." She paused to listen. "No, she's conscious now. She seems like she's okay." She listened again then nodded. "Okay." She put her hand over the mouthpiece and glanced at us. "Lock the doors."

Harvey ran out to the front, and Carly stepped over to the back door I'd just come in and turned the dead bolt.

I hugged myself, rubbing the goose bumps

on my arms.

Harvey came back in and pulled Alice to him. "Door's locked out there," he said softly.

She nodded, still holding the phone to her ear, occasionally murmuring to the emergency operator to let her know we were all still okay.

Vini, his arms crossed, stood in front of the sink, facing me. The fear in his eyes was like the measles, contagious and uncomfortable. I glanced away to where Debbie stood beside me, holding gentle pressure on the frozen peas at the back of my head and texting on her cell phone with her other hand.

Carly patted my shoulder, and I covered her hand with mine. No one spoke.

She squeezed my hand then stepped over to the stove, lifted the lid off the bean soup, and gave it an absent stir.

"You know if you stir it much after it's been cooking awhile, it'll be bean mush instead of soup," Alice said.

Carly dropped the lid.

"No, ma'am," Alice said into the phone. "I wasn't talking to you."

A siren in the distance cut off whatever Carly might have been going to say. The wailing quickly grew louder.

Red lights flashed through the kitchen window that faced the alley. I had a sinking feeling the ambulance crew was too late for the guy in the car. Almost immediately, blue lights mixed with the red. And still more blue lights.

Alice nudged Harvey. "She says to go let the police in the front door."

Harvey hurried out, and within seconds he was back with two local officers, Seth and Ricky, behind him.

Alice hung up the phone.

"Jenna, you okay?" Seth asked, concern evident in his voice.

I nodded. Debbie took the peas from my head and went to put them back in the freezer.

"You sure?" Seth said.

"I've got a little bump, but other than that, I think I'll live." *Unlike the guy in the alley.* I shivered.

Seth and I had a history. When I first moved back to town and was trying my hand at dating, he'd asked me out — then promptly killed the romance when he assumed that he'd get to work out at the gym for free if we were dating. In light of the dead body out back, that little breach of etiquette didn't stop me from being happy to see him. Or his partner, Ricky, either, in spite of the frown he wore and the notebook he pulled from his back pocket.

"What happened out there?" Ricky asked, the hand holding the pen a little unsteady and a slight quiver in his voice. I had the distinct feeling this was his first murder.

Seth cut him a look and brought his gaze back to me. "Do we need the EMTs in here?"

I shook my head, and at the movement, my hand flew up to cup the lump on the back of my skull. "Ow."

"Get someone in here to look at her," Seth growled over his shoulder to Ricky.

The tall cop put his notebook away then disappeared into the diner.

Seth pulled up a chair next to me and sat down. "You look pretty pale. Is it bleeding?"

"I don't think so." I ducked my head.

He carefully parted my hair and grunted. "No blood, but that's a prize-winning goose egg."

"Thanks," I said dryly. "It's nice to be a winner."

"You're always a winner to me."

Something in his voice brought my gaze around to meet his.

He smiled. "You still dating Alex?"

"Last time I checked she was engaged to him," a deep voice said behind me.

I turned toward the familiar voice. Alex Campbell filled the doorway, his face taut with worry. "You okay?"

I nodded, so glad to see him I couldn't speak.

He covered the distance between us in two strides and bent down to hug me.

Seth jumped to his feet and took a couple steps backward. He even held out his hand as if offering Alex his vacated chair. Alex had been the high school quarterback when Seth was a lowly tenth-grade bench warmer. Old habits die hard.

"Thanks," Alex mumbled, his attention still fixed on me. He released me as he sat down but held on to my hand.

A female EMT came bustling in, her black bag in her hand. She checked my vision and examined the lump on my head. When she finished, she looked at Alex and smiled. "Everything looks okay to me. But you probably want to get her over to the ER to get this checked out. A hit hard enough to knock someone out usually causes a concussion."

Hello? I started to wave my hand to remind her who was the patient here. But I was too tired. I was used to this phenomenon when I was out with the town's most eligible bachelor. Even my new engagement ring hadn't seemed to slow the attention down much. I glanced over at Debbie. Tonight the waitress was more interested in her cell phone, but usually she spoke to Alex instead of me. In Alex's defense, though, he always kept his own gaze fixed on me — which was one of the many things I loved about him.

As soon as the EMT left, Alex turned me to face him. "What happened, honey?"

"Might as well just tell it once, 'honey,' " someone said gruffly.

I looked up to see our chief of police standing in the suddenly popular doorway. "Hi, John." We'd been friends since the sandbox, but my penchant for sniffing out the truth drove him up the wall sometimes.

"You know, Jenna, it'd be funny if it weren't so horrible." He walked in with Ricky right behind him.

Fresh tears sprang to my eyes. "I know." It hadn't been long since I found the queen of country music dead in her Branson dressing room, and less than a year before that, I'd gotten embroiled in the murder of our local newspaper editor. So I knew what he meant.

"You all right?"

"I guess. Physically, anyway."

"What is it with you and dead bodies?"

I shrugged, and an involuntary shiver ran up my spine. Alex put his arm around me and pulled me against him.

"I —"

John held up his hand. "Forget I asked. Let's just concentrate on this one. Tell me about finding the body."

"I was taking out the trash," I stammered. "It was almost closing time." I glanced at Carly.

She nodded. "It was right at eight o'clock. We only had a few stragglers when you went out." Her face flushed, and she spoke to John. "We were busy cleaning, so we didn't notice when she didn't come back right away." She flashed me an apologetic look.

He waved away her implied apology and turned his shrewd gaze back to me. "So what happened when you got out there?"

I told him as coherently as I could. Ricky scribbled in his little notebook while I talked.

"You felt for a pulse?" John said, looking at my apron.

I glanced down and froze at the sight of the rusty fingerprints. Apparently I'd instinctively wiped the blood off before I was clobbered. I clutched Alex's hand tightly and nodded. "Then something hit me in the head from behind."

"Did you lose consciousness immediately?"

"I must have. I don't remember anything after that until I woke up staring at a tire."

"What time did you come back in here?"

I glanced at Debbie, who shook her head. Then Vini, Harvey, Alice, and Carly. They all looked stricken. "It couldn't have been more than fifteen minutes after eight," Carly said.

Vini pointed at Alice. "She called emergency. They will know what time, yes?"

"Yes," John agreed. "So right after you came in, they called 911?"

"Well, once someone noticed me," I said, irritated at the whine in my voice. Still, it had been disconcerting not to be missed. "Debbie got me some frozen peas."

I looked over at Debbie, who was leaning against the wall typing on her cell phone. She didn't even look up at me.

John's brows drew together. "Frozen peas?"

"For my head. But within two minutes, I'd say, Alice called."

John looked at Ricky. "Get me the time of that 911 call."

Ricky nodded and disappeared.

John turned back to us. "Had anyone else been out back before that?"

Everyone shook their heads, then Alice glanced up at Harvey. "Wait. Harv, you took the trash out about twenty minutes before Jenna did, remember?"

John fixed his gaze on Harvey, who nodded.

"Did you see a car behind the Dumpster?"

"I didn't look behind the Dumpster. I knew if I didn't hurry back in" — he glanced at Vini — "the salad bar would be in shambles. I just tossed the trash."

I spoke up. "I wouldn't have noticed the car if one of my bags hadn't gone over and landed on its roof."

Alice took Harvey's arm and put it around her. "Just think, honey. There may have been a murderer right next to you." She frowned. "It's scary to think he was out there with you, Jenna."

"Yeah, scary." I gently touched the goose egg on the back of my head and looked down at my skinned knees. "And painful."

"Do you know the guy's name?" Debbie asked softly, slipping her phone into her apron pocket. From the drawn look on her face, the text conversation hadn't gone well.

John nodded. "J. D. Finley."

Debbie gasped. A couple of other people made noises, but I couldn't be sure who. All of us looked at Debbie. Her face matched her white apron, and tears threatened to ruin her freshly applied makeup.

"I take it you know him?" John said.

She nodded and bit her lower lip. "He's a friend of Lisa's. They've been dating for a while, I guess." She tried to wipe the tears away with one finger, but they tumbled down her cheeks anyway. "I've been out with them a few times."

John gave her a stern look that I knew meant there would be more questions for her later.

She shrugged. "Poor Lisa. This will break her heart." The last word became a quiet sob. Carly handed her a paper towel.

Bob's daughter was lucky to have a friend like Debbie. As far as I knew, few people but her parents would have cared if it were Lisa herself who was out in that car in the alley.

John turned to the rest of us. "What do the rest of you know about him?"

Harvey nodded toward Alice as he answered for both of them. "We knew him."

"Was he in here tonight?" John asked.

"I didn't see him," Debbie said, but didn't look up.

"Me, either," Harvey said. "And I was working the cash register by the front door, so if he'd been in here, I'd have known it."

"Anyone know what he was doing out in the alley?" John asked us all.

No one answered. Finally, Alice spoke up. "Maybe he was supposed to meet Lisa? I mean, if they were dating, maybe they arranged a date here."

I shook my head. "Why would he have parked behind the trash bin to meet Lisa here for a date? That makes no sense."

John apparently agreed with me. He frowned. "Anyone see Lisa here tonight?"

We all shook our heads. Considering I quit my job and gave up my dream of owning the Lake View Athletic Club because of her, I was pretty sure I'd have noticed if my nemesis had been here.

Seth motioned to John from the doorway.

"Be right there."

Seth nodded and disappeared into the dining room. John turned back to us. "If I think of anything else I need to ask, I'll call you."

"Wait. John." I touched his sleeve. "Who is J. D. Finley? Is he from around here?"

"Jenna, I'm sure we'll find out all there is to know about him before this is over, but this is official police business. You need to let us do our job." The "and stay out of it" was implied as he turned toward the door.

"I think finding a dead body puts me right

in the middle of it."

He sighed. "Just this once, can't you mind your own business?"

Alex shifted in his chair to look at me. "I'll be right back, hon. I'm gonna ask John a couple of questions. Will you be okay?" When I nodded, he rose, and together he and the chief strode out of the kitchen.

I stood and walked to the staff bathroom to check out my head. No matter how I contorted, I couldn't see the bump, but I could feel it. I blinked my eyes. No double vision. I didn't feel particularly sleepy. And other than feeling a little disoriented from finding a dead body, I wasn't dizzy. I washed my hands and opened the door.

"Surely you know I wouldn't blame you," Alice said as I stepped back into the kitchen.

She and Harvey looked at me and froze.

3

As nervous as a long-tailed cat
in a room full of rocking chairs

Harvey's face lost most of its color, but he laughed. "It wouldn't be the first time you've accused me of turning the burner up under your soup," he said.

Alice's answering chuckle sounded forced. "Of course, you're right. But I'm not accusing you this time. Just saying that I wouldn't blame you if you had turned the burner up in all this excitement."

"I didn't," he said firmly.

"That's fine," she said.

I smiled weakly and walked into the dining room where everyone else had gathered. Whatever that had been about, it wasn't soup.

Carly looked at me as I walked in. "You want me to go to the ER with you?"

"No, I'm fine. I'm going to stay and help

you clean up."

"You most certainly are not," Carly said. Alex and John moved closer as if they were her strongmen ready to enforce her decree.

"I will help clean," Vini offered.

Carly smiled at the twentysomething Albanian. "Thanks. And Elliott's supposed to stop by and help, too." She turned back to me. "Go get your head checked out. We've got this covered."

"I'll just go home and rest then. The EMT checked me out, and I don't have any signs of a concussion."

I'd expected an argument from Alex, but before he could say anything, John put his hand on my arm. "I think you should go on down to the ER."

I smiled. "You, of all people, should know how hard my head is."

He frowned. "I can't believe you're joking. You could have been killed."

"Aw, it's nice to know you care."

Alex snorted. John and I had never really outgrown our childhood "one up" type of friendship. Bless her heart, my friend Denise, who married the big lout, always ended up having to mediate.

John shot me a wry grin. "Truth is, Denise would kill *me* if anything happened to you on my watch. If you have any symptoms, you go get it checked out." He sauntered over to where Ricky and Seth were sitting at a booth looking at Ricky's notebook.

As we walked out of the diner, Alex kept his arm around my waist. "You know, in spite of his gruff talk, he thinks of you as a little sister."

"Yeah, an annoying little sister that he wishes he could box up and ship to Siberia."

Alex laughed. "I'm glad to see you getting back to normal. You were pretty pale when I got here."

"Getting conked on the head tends to do that to a person."

His smile disappeared. "You speak from entirely too much experience on that subject."

"Found another body, did you?" The old man from the feed store on Main Street gave me a snaggletoothed grin.

"Yep." I gritted my own full set of teeth into some semblance of a smile and tapped my order pad with my pencil. "What can I get for you today?"

"I'll have the meatloaf special. Gettin' to be a habit of yours, idn't it? Gettin' involved with murder? I'm surprised you're not out back helping the police look for the gun."

His cronies laughed.

"Hush up, Grimmett," Marge Templeton scolded from the booth across the way. "Jenna can't help being in the wrong place at the wrong time."

"Grimmett" ducked his head, his weathered face mottled with embarrassment. Apparently he hadn't realized that Marge was nearby. Her late husband, Hank, had been my first "wrong place at the wrong time." Even though I hadn't actually found the newspaper editor's body, I'd eventually solved his murder. Sort of. And almost gotten myself and Carly killed in the process.

I gave Marge a grateful glance. We shared a bond of having been in a sticky situation together. I knew I could count on her to watch my back. She owned the paper now, and although it wasn't common knowledge, she was also my boss. She and her niece, the new editor, were the only two people besides Carly and me who knew that I moonlighted as advice columnist Dear Pru.

The other old-timers told me what they wanted to eat without incident. As I wove my way through the busy dining area with their orders, I admitted to myself that Grimmett was right about one thing: I'd much rather be out back with the police looking for the gun that killed J.D. But I had sense enough to know John would come unglued if I got anywhere near them.

"Ma'am! Ma'am!" A big-haired lady on the opposite side of the room waved her arm. "This isn't what I ordered."

I glanced around the busy dining area. Where was Debbie?

I made a quick detour to the woman's table, and she gestured toward her plate. "I know you aren't our waitress, but ours seems to have disappeared. I ordered a salad and chopped steak. This is meatloaf."

I took the offending plate. "I'm sorry, ma'am. I'll be right back with your salad."

"Thanks. I heard y'all talking about that guy that was killed here last night. Wasn't he from here originally?"

I shook my head. "Not that I know of."

She nodded to the mousy-looking woman across the table from her. "Didn't your grandma say he grew up here?"

"Yes," the woman said.

"I hadn't heard that." And as much as I wanted to hear more, I knew I needed to find Debbie before Carly lost customers because her wait staff was too slow. "I'll just go get your order."

I leaned over the counter into the kitchen to see if Debbie was in there. All I could see was orders piling up. I glanced over to the salad bar where Vini was dumping fresh lettuce into the huge stainless steel bowl. "Vini, I think Debbie must be on break. Can you help me serve for a few minutes?"

For the next half hour, we worked frantically, sorting out orders and making corrections and apologies.

When the lunch crowd thinned slightly, I thanked Vini. "Can you handle things out here for a few minutes while I find Debbie?"

He nodded.

I looked in the kitchen and even opened the mop closet. But no Debbie. Finally, I went to the ladies' room and peeked in. Empty. I started to let the door shut, but a muffled sobbing drew me back. "Debbie?"

Just a soft hiccup in answer.

"Debbie? Is that you?" I glanced under the stall and saw her scuffed white tennis shoes, still slightly speckled with the butternut paint from the remodel. "I know it's you. You might as well talk to me."

She blew her nose loudly, and in a few seconds the stall door creaked open and she stepped out.

"What's wrong?" I asked.

"This whole murder thing. I just feel bad about J.D. It's so sad." She bent over the sink and splashed cold water on her red, puffy face.

I met her gaze in the mirror. "It is. Do you have any idea who might have killed him?"

"No, of course not. I barely knew him." Her voice quavered, and she fished her brush out of her purse and redid her messy bun. "But poor Lisa."

"Yeah." I thought again how lucky Lisa was to have Debbie for a friend. Most people in Lake View probably wouldn't have too much sympathy for the spoiled princess. "Do you know why he was here?"

She shrugged. "How would I know? Maybe he was coming to the grand opening." Her voice broke. "But he didn't make it." She began sobbing again.

I patted her shoulder. "Debbie, why don't you go ahead and go home? Vini and I can handle the rest of the lunch crowd." It would be easier if we knew she was gone than if she kept disappearing to cry. I hoped Carly wouldn't care that I was sending her most seasoned waitress home during the busiest part of the day. "If you feel like it, you can come back in later."

"I don't want to go home."

"Then maybe you should visit Lisa. I'm sure she's having a hard time with this."

She nodded. "I heard they made her go

down to the station this morning and have fingerprints," she whispered.

Her unique way of phrasing that procedure made me fight a smile. "Really? They think she killed him?"

Her eyes widened. "Do you think? They said it's just a formality because she rode in his car a lot. So they can figure out what fingerprints might be there that aren't supposed to be."

I quickly backtracked. The last thing I wanted to do was add to the overworked rumor mill. "No, no, I'm sure she's not a suspect. Eliminating fingerprints that belong there sounds right. And anyway, why would she kill her new boyfriend?"

Debbie's eyes filled with tears again. "Relationships can be hard."

"Yeah, I know. But even though 'breaking up is hard to do,' don't you think it would be harder to kill him?"

She pulled a tissue from the holder on the counter and loudly blew her nose again instead of answering. Should I have mentioned that was a rhetorical question?

I patted her on the shoulder. My mother and Carly were so much better than I was at sympathy and advice. Why did I always end up in these situations? "I'll tell Carly that you're taking the rest of the day off."

"Thanks." She gave a wan smile and left.

I hurried back to the dining room. From the corner of my eye, I saw Harvey directing a couple toward one of my tables. I grabbed two menus and headed over to take their orders. As I neared the table, I recognized Seth's partner, Ricky, and Tiffany Stanton, the mayor's daughter. Tiffany had moved back to Lake View only a few months ago to take a job as editor of her aunt's newspaper, and Ricky hadn't wasted any time in getting to know her. When the tall cop wasn't on duty, you could always count on seeing them together.

Since her parents, Amelia and Byron, sent her to boarding school instead of Lake View High, I hadn't known Tiffany well when we were growing up. But I'd always thought of her as the Anti-Amelia. She had pretty features, but it almost seemed like she did everything she could to hide them. Her naturally curly hair frizzed around her bare face, and she usually wore shapeless clothes or men's jeans that did nothing to flatter her figure.

Today, even though she hadn't changed a thing, she looked as radiant as a bride. "What'll you have to drink?" My standard opening line.

"What are you having, Ricky?" She leaned

52

toward him. "Sweet tea with lemon?"

He grinned. "You know me too well."

She beamed at me. "I'll have the same." She waved her hand in the air, and I could tell she was showing off the huge rock on her engagement finger.

When I brought the drinks back, they thanked me.

I pulled out my order pad. "Congratulations on your engagement. Your ring is beautiful. Is the wedding soon?"

"Yes." Tiffany flashed Ricky a coy look. "We don't want a long engagement, do we, honey?"

He ducked his head. "The sooner the better."

She scooted closer and kissed him on the cheek. "We're hoping to get married next month. Although . . ." She pursed her lips as if she had tasted the lemon from her sweet tea. "*Mother* says she doesn't see how we can possibly be ready in a month."

I could understand that. My own wedding was scheduled for Christmas, and even though it was going to be small, I had a checklist that was quickly looming out of control.

"Speaking of your mother," Ricky murmured and stood as Amelia and Byron Stanton walked toward us. I quickly grabbed two more menus while he pulled out Amelia's chair for her to sit down.

I took the mayor and first lady's drink order and hurried away. A few minutes later, as I carefully set the drinks on the table, I glanced at Tiffany. The change was amazing. Her arms were crossed defensively in front of her, and the radiance was gone. "I think you just don't want me to get married." She glared sullenly at her mother. "You've never really wanted me to be happy."

Amelia glanced up at me and gave a nervous laugh. "Honey, of course I want you to be happy. I just think you're rushing this." She looked to Byron as if for support. "We want you to have a wedding to remember, and that takes some time to plan. You don't want off-the-rack dresses for the bridesmaids, do you? And what about your gown?" I'd often thought Amelia was like a Barbie doll with no real feelings or emotions, but her distress was very real.

I took my pad and pen out of my apron. "Have y'all decided what you want to eat?" I asked in my most cheerful voice, then motioned Vanna-like toward the white dry-erase board on the wall. "These are today's specials."

Amelia ignored my motion and glanced

down at the menu in her hand. "I'll have the chef salad with blue cheese dressing on the side." She looked at me over her menu. "Carly does make her own salad dressing, doesn't she?"

"Yes, of course. I'm partial to her honey mustard, but the blue cheese is great, too."

Tiffany didn't look at the white board, either. Carly was going to fire me if I didn't do a better job of promoting the already-made food.

"I'll have a cheeseburger and fries off the menu." Tiffany smiled at Ricky. "That's what you want, too, isn't it, baby?"

"Sure is." He patted her on the hand. "You always know just what I like."

I saw Amelia's jaw muscle jump as she gritted her teeth. Was her son-in-law-to-be needling her on purpose?

"And you, Mayor Stanton?"

"I'll have the chicken-fried steak and gravy, mashed potatoes, and fried okra."

Thank you, Mr. Mayor. Finally, someone who was ordering one of the specials. Maybe my job was safe for another day.

Later, when I set the serving tray beside their table and began unloading it, they were still discussing the upcoming nuptials.

"We do have an image to uphold, dear." Amelia was again speaking through gritted teeth. She was going to need dental work if she kept this up. "We can't just throw something together, especially if your dad is going to run for the senate." She lowered her voice on the last three words.

Debbie had warned me that as a waitress I would hear lots of personal business and gossip. "We're like the furniture," she'd said. And it looked like she was right.

I set their plates in front of them and headed back to pick up an order for another table. I got busy with my other tables but stopped back by to see if they needed refills.

Ricky pushed to his feet just as I approached. "I'm going to go out and see if I can help the guys," he said as he threw a couple of ones on the table and handed a twenty to Tiffany. "Do you mind handling our bill, honey?"

She shook her head and shoved the money back to him. "Today's my treat."

He glanced at her parents then back at her and frowned. "I'd rather pay for it, okay?" he said quietly.

She glared at her mother then nodded. "Sure, sweetie." She took the twenty-dollar bill. When he was gone, she turned to her mother. "I hope you're happy. You ran him off."

Amelia's elaborately made-up eyes widened. "Why, Tiffany, I did no such thing."

"You know what? I need to go. I'll talk to y'all later." Tiffany dropped a kiss on Byron's forehead, and with barely a glance at her mother, stomped up to the cash register.

Byron stood and retrieved his and Amelia's bill. "I'm going to go on and pay, too." He followed his daughter.

"Well, at least she didn't eat all of that fat-filled burger," Amelia murmured as I refilled her glass.

Indignant on Carly's behalf, I protested. "That's ground chuck —"

Amelia waved her hand. "Never mind, dear. I need a favor."

"A 'to go' box?"

She frowned, but thanks to one-too-many Botox treatments, only her eyes showed it. "No, silly." She glanced at her husband and daughter and lowered her voice. "You're so good at snooping. I need you to find out what you can about Ricky before he and Tiffany get married." She was talking so fast and quietly, I could barely understand her. "We had her last boyfriend investigated. It turned out badly, and she was broken-hearted for a while." She sipped her tea and lifted her hand in a lazy wave to a nearby diner. "We don't want that to happen again," she said to me from the corner of her mouth.

"You know, Amelia, I'm not a PI. Can't you just have a professional check him out, run a background check, that kind of thing?"

She put her hand to her heart as if I'd suggested having him murdered. "No. Tiffany made us promise not to do that ever again."

Maybe she wasn't as managing a mother as I thought.

Her next words dispelled that delusion. "I'd do it anyway, but I'm afraid she would find out." She took a drink. "But you can do it. You ask questions all the time, anyway, so no one would think it was odd."

Thanks a lot.

"Besides, you know John and Seth both. They'll tell you anything." Ha, little did she know. John wouldn't tell me the time of day unless he had to. Well, he wasn't that bad, but he certainly didn't share information with me.

"I guess I can ask them about him. If you really want me to. But he seems like a regular guy to me. Why are you so worried?"

"Tiffany doesn't attract men like some girls do." She glanced at me. "Well, look at her. No wonder she doesn't. I could have helped her, but from the time she was small, if I even made a suggestion about her looks or clothes, she took it as an insult."

Amelia looked toward the door where Byron motioned toward her that he was ready. "Anyway, she hasn't had good luck with men. Ricky seems fine, but we just want to make sure. Will you do it?"

"I don't know . . ."

She tapped her nails impatiently on the table. "I seem to remember I didn't hesitate when you asked me to look into something for you."

I shrugged. What could I say? She was right. In the last murder I'd been investigating, I'd asked her to check something out and she had. "I'll figure out a way to ask John and Seth what they think about him without seeming suspicious. And I'll let you know."

She pulled out a ten-dollar bill and left it on the table. "Thanks."

I scooped the ten into my apron pocket and watched the first lady of Lake View glide across the room.

Poor Ricky. He had no idea what he was getting into.

4

A watched pot never boils.

Within five minutes, Harvey was ringing up the last few stragglers from the lunch crowd. I was learning the ebb and flow of customers. They all came at once. They all left at once.

I walked over to where Alice carefully filled the saltshakers.

She smiled at me. "I bet you're worn out. Not bein' used to this and all."

I didn't know it showed. Every part of me was longing for a nice, relaxing swim in the club pool. I would've even settled for taking inventory or cleaning the equipment in the exercise room. I sank into a chair and groaned. "My feet may never be the same. I don't see how you've done this for so long. No wonder you wanted to sell this place."

A cloud crossed her face. "It's never easy making a change, though. We've lived in

Lake View our whole lives. And Harvey's parents owned the diner before us."

I needed a new subject fast. "I heard today that J. D. Finley was from here when he was young. Is that true?"

"Um-hum," she grunted without looking up.

I waited for her to elaborate, but she concentrated on sifting the tiny white granules into the last shaker.

She finished and picked up the big plastic pitcher full of salt. "With all those police officers out back, I'd better go see about the pies I have in the oven."

I stared at her back. If I wanted to snoop, I was going to have to find someone more loquacious than Alice.

Or — I glanced out at the parking lot where police cars were parked everywhere — I could see for myself what was going on.

I stood and stretched then ambled into the kitchen and poured a cup of coffee. "I'm on break," I called to Carly as I let myself quietly out the back door, clutching my mug casually. No law against an overworked waitress taking a break out back, was there?

Across the small alley the infamous Dumpster loomed. Behind it and to the sides were scraggly woods — land that had probably been cleared less than a decade ago but had been ignored since. Today that little thicket was literally crawling with cops.

I leaned against the wooden post and watched the search.

"Spread out more," John barked, and the officers quickly obeyed.

Thankfully no one even looked my way, or our esteemed chief of police certainly would have ordered me back inside.

Just as I drained the last drop of my coffee, an excited yell went up from an area on the very outskirts of the woods.

I stood on my tiptoes and could make out two familiar figures. "Over here!" Seth and Ricky waved their arms. "Found it!"

Lake View's police force descended on them en masse, no doubt trampling significant clues in the process.

I heard John growling at them, so apparently he thought the same thing. Within seconds, they headed back in my direction, John carrying a plastic bag with something small in it. As he drew closer, I squinted at the contents. Undoubtedly a gun, but it looked more like a tiny water pistol. Hard to believe something so small could do so much damage.

Before I could slip back inside, John spotted me. His face grew red, and he twisted his mouth as if trying to think of what to say, but he just sputtered.

I held my hand up in an international gesture of peace. "I'm going, I'm going."

I quickly let myself back into the diner before my childhood friend had a coronary. Sometimes he really overreacted to my tendency to want to know what was going on.

"Wow, Carly. You're a genius." I wiggled my toes in the warm water. "I'm so glad you bought two."

"I can't take credit. I got them because of the advice Alice gave me." Carly sank down in her own chair and immersed her feet in the plastic foot spa in front of her. She groaned and closed her eyes. " 'Take good care of your feet,' she said. 'And they'll take good care of you.' "

"Speaking of Alice . . ." I couldn't believe I'd been so drained that I'd forgotten this. "Yesterday after John let us all go, I over-heard Alice say something odd to Harvey."

"She says odd things to him all the time," Carly said without opening her eyes.

"Yeah, but she said, 'I wouldn't blame you.' Or something like that."

She sat up. "For what?"

I shrugged. "She *said* for turning the

burner up under the soup."

"Oh. Well, the soup was a little scorched today, I thought. Maybe that's all it was."

"Maybe."

For a few minutes we sat, without speaking, in the darkened living room of the small cabin on our folks' property that Carly and the kids had moved into a few months ago. With the girls in bed, Zac in his room on the phone, and our heated foot spas bubbling, we'd created a relaxation haven.

"I guess you don't think it was a stranger this time, either, do you?" Carly said tiredly.

I didn't even have to wonder for a second what she meant. "I wish I did, but not really." Each time we'd gotten embroiled in a murder, we'd tried to cling to the false hope that the killer was a stranger. Both of the other two times we'd been sadly disappointed.

"Yeah, me either. One can only hold on to that kind of naïveté for so long."

I squinted toward her. "Aren't you getting cynical?"

She shrugged. "Having a dead man show up at your grand opening tends to do that to you."

"Excuse me for ruining your grand opening by finding a body," I said. "Why do you think he was there?"

Carly kept her head resting against the padded back of her chair. "Well, since I already sound like a narcissist, maybe someone hired him to sabotage my big day."

I snorted. "No doubt. Wonder what the pay is for that?" I asked. "Dying in order to sabotage?"

She snorted back at me without opening her eyes. "Okay then, smarty. I guess it would be too flippant to say that he might have put out a hit on himself to get him out of his relationship with Lisa."

I reached over and shoved her gently. "I think we've officially come down with the eleven o'clock sillies."

"Mama always says the only cure for that is going to bed before eleven," Carly said in a pseudoserious tone.

"Well, Mama should have come over and helped us clean up tonight at the diner," I spouted. "Then we wouldn't be so tired we can't sleep."

"Good point," she murmured.

"I know the difference," I said suddenly.

"Difference in what?" Carly asked, something in my voice alerting her that my silliness had vanished. She sat up and looked over at me.

"This body. This time we don't know the victim. So we have no idea who might have done it."

"Very true," Carly said thoughtfully. "And since he was in fact a *stranger* to us . . ."

"A stranger might very well have killed him," I finished triumphantly, feeling a little rejuvenated at the thought. "And we don't even have to know why."

"Sunday dinner at your mom's," Alex said with a sigh as he helped me clear the table. "One of the many things I missed all those years we were apart."

I waved a fork at him. "You only love me for my mama's cooking?" I teased. "We may have a problem."

He nudged me and motioned to Carly and Elliott, who still sat whispering with their heads together at the other end of the long table. "You think *we* have a problem? At least *we* know the meal is over."

Elliott looked up and grinned. "Hey now, we're not deaf."

"Well, stop the mushiness then, Romeo. You're making me look bad." Alex returned his grin.

Carly laughed. "This from the man who had my sister swept away in a limo to meet him for a private dinner at the marina."

"And then bought her a rock the size of Manhattan a few weeks later," Elliott chimed in.

"And even more romantically, helps me with the dishes," I said, winking at Alex.

"I think that was a hint for us to get busy." Elliott stood and pulled Carly to her feet then put his arm around her and pulled her close. He whispered something in her ear.

The twins came running in, followed by Zac.

"Mom, can we go now?" Hayley's query was more of a command.

"Yeah," Rachel chimed in. "You said as soon as lunch was over we could go get ready for the basketball game."

"Pipe down, kiddos." Zac spoiled his big-brother attitude by adding, "But everyone's goin' down to the courts soon, right, Mom? I want to practice my jump shot before the game starts." He turned to Elliott. "Can't you make her hurry?"

"Hurry a woman? Son, you've got lots to learn" — Elliott winked at Zac — "but I'll do what I can."

"Out!" I made shooing motions at the kids. Then I stopped. "On second thought, why don't you take these dirty dishes in the kitchen and tell your grandma that y'all will load the dishwasher? When you finish, we'll show you who the athletes really are."

"I'll show them how to hold down a lawn

chair," Carly muttered.

The kids obediently took all the dishes and exited the dining room, but they were so busy laughing about our supposed athletic ability that Hayley bumped into the door facing. Served her right.

Forty-five minutes later, we were waiting for a few stragglers on the concrete basketball court just past the playground. One of the benefits of being raised at a resort — plenty of room for friendly games. And plenty of extra players. Just as Dad finished going over the rules, the honeymooners in cabin five came running up. "Are we too late?"

Dad shook his head. "The cops are just now getting here." He motioned to where the black-and-white patrol car had pulled into a parking place.

The man stopped in his tracks and put a protective arm around his new wife. "Excuse me?"

Dad laughed and pointed at John, Ricky, and Seth, who were walking across the gravel parking lot toward us. "Don't worry, son. The chief of police has a mean three-pointer, but he isn't worth a dime on defense. And that tall cop gets all the rebounds, but when he shoots, you don't need to worry. He can't hit the broad side of the barn. And Seth? Well, he's just Seth. You'll see."

Everyone laughed, even the newcomers.

A new hybrid vehicle pulled in and bypassed the parking lot, driving across the gravel directly to the basketball court. Before I could guess who the driver might be, Tiffany Stanton emerged. She waved and smiled then walked around the car and opened the passenger door. John's wife, Denise, climbed out, her usually slender frame struggling to hold the extra twenty-five pounds she had gained in the first eight months of her pregnancy. They already had two children, but this was Denise's first pregnancy since turning thirty. John had apparently read that with age came danger. He'd been treating Denise as if she were made of spun gold for the last several months.

The cops had almost reached us when John heard us greet Tiffany and Denise behind him. He spun around to look. "What is she doing here? I told her she needed to rest."

He hurried over to Denise and cupped her elbow with his hand. I would be annoyed by the constant attention, but Denise seemed to be coping very well. Then again, looks could be deceiving. Even though she

69

smiled as she struggled to gain her balance, there was a hint of gritted teeth in the smile. She waved and began walking toward us with John scampering around her like an overgrown puppy.

"I'm okay, John. I needed to get out of the house, and your mom volunteered to babysit." Denise's words floated to us, her exasperation clear in her tone. "I can walk by myself. Why don't you get my chair out of the car?"

Tiffany had opened the trunk, and she stepped back to let John take the red lawn chair. Ricky waved her over to be on his team, and she jogged toward him.

I'd never have thought of her as athletic, but then again she was the opposite of her mother, and I sure couldn't imagine Amelia enjoying a pick-up basketball game or hanging out at the Stafford Cabins play area on a Sunday afternoon, for that matter.

We all stood there gawking at the John and Denise show as they reached us and he got her settled into her chair. By the time he had her situated to suit him, she almost needed binoculars to keep up with the action. He handed her his phone and his portable radio and turned toward us.

As soon as he finished, Dad said, "Denise, you can be on my team. We need a good guard." He winked at me.

Sure enough, John rose to the bait. "She can't play!" As we burst out laughing, he grinned weakly. "Oh, I guess you knew that."

"Go on, honey, you play and uphold the family honor," Denise said, edging her chair closer to where Carly, Mama, and the twins were sitting. "I'll just watch safely from the sidelines and cheer you on."

After the kayaker from cabin seven joined us, we had twelve players, just enough for three teams of four. We flipped a coin to see who would play the first round. Seth, Ricky, Tiffany, and John drew the first game against Alex, Elliot, Zac, and me. That left Dad, the honeymooners, and the kayaker for the third team.

During a water break, Tiffany and I joined Carly, Mama, and Denise on the sidelines.

"Nice shooting there, Tex," I drawled to Tiffany.

She smiled. "Two years of dating a basketball coach. He was obsessed with the game, and if I wanted to see him, it had to be on the court."

When we went back onto the court, the game moved fast and furiously. We were up by six points when Seth went up for a shot. He missed, but as he came down, he yelled,

"Foul!" at Alex.

Alex frowned. "I don't think so."

Ricky walked up to stand beside Seth. "Think so or not, you did," he said to Alex.

"We'll replay." Alex offered a compromise.

Seth shrugged. "Fine by me."

Before we could resume play, though, Denise hollered for John. He gasped and sprinted toward her, no doubt expecting to have to deliver the baby right there on the sidelines. But she waggled his cell phone at him.

We all sat down on the concrete for a short break while he took the call. Zac, Elliott, Alex, and I sat together.

"You didn't foul him," Zac murmured.

Alex shrugged. "It's just a game."

Elliott smiled. "Easy to say when we're ahead."

Zac's face brightened. "We are smoking them, aren't we?"

Elliott nodded. "Nice three-pointer, buddy."

"Thanks. I've been practicing."

I had a flash of realization. Carly was incredibly blessed that Zac and Elliott had such an easy relationship. Amelia and Tiffany were proof that even a blood bond didn't guarantee that kind of camaraderie.

John clicked his phone shut and walked

back over to the court. "Seth, Ricky, I need you to come with me. Something's come up. Good game, y'all." The last was aimed at us as the men headed purposefully to John's car. I dashed after them and tried to casually stroll along beside John. Kind of hard since he took one step to my two.

"John, are you going to the station?"

He kept walking.

"Did someone have a wreck? Is anyone hurt?"

Still walking.

But my gut wouldn't let me be quiet. "This has something to do with the murder case, hasn't it?"

No answer.

"John Connor, you make me so mad. All you have to do is tell me what's going on."

Finally, he whipped his head around to look at me. "You're wrong there, Jenna. I don't have to tell you anything. This is official police business. Go play ball."

After the third game, which, by the way, we won handily, the guests went back to their own cabins and the rest of us scattered. Carly and Elliott headed out to the glider under the elm tree. Alex had some work to catch up on, so Mama and I walked over to the porch swing.

"Mama, did you know the guy that was

murdered was from here?" I sat down in the swing.

She sat down beside me. "Yes."

"Did you and Daddy know him?" I pushed off the swing with my toe.

"We knew who he was. He left here a long time ago."

"Tell me about him. Where did he go?"

"I don't know all that much about him, honey. And I have no idea where he went."

"I just want to know why he was killed. And who murdered him."

"Honey . . ." Mama pushed the swing with her foot. "I know you. The more you learn, the more you want to find out. And before you know it, you're right in the middle of a murder investigation."

There was definitely truth in what she was saying, but it still stung. "C'mon, it happened right there behind the diner. Plus I found the body." I shivered involuntarily. "It's not like I chose this."

"No, but you choose whether or not to get involved. You know I've always said your curiosity would be your downfall." She turned to look at me. "And so far you've managed to survive, but I pray every day that you'll be safe."

"I appreciate it." I pushed the swing gently. "That's probably what's kept me alive this long." I grinned in an effort to lighten things up a little.

She answered my grin with a frown. "Just wait until you have kids of your own. You've never worried until you've worried about your children." She stopped the swing with her foot and turned toward me. "Your daddy and I want you to promise to stay out of it this time."

"I understand." I wasn't making any promises, except one to myself to keep my mama and daddy from worrying about me.

She reached over and patted my hand. "We're just tired of visiting you in the hospital."

Across the yard, a motion caught our attention. Carly jumped up out of the glider and stomped toward the back of the house. Elliott got up and followed her. She turned and said something that we couldn't hear and waved him away. He walked slowly with his head down toward his car.

I looked back at Mama. "Do you think we should go after her?"

"No. What did I tell you about minding your own business? If she wants to tell us she will."

But I couldn't help noticing the worried expression on Mama's face.

5

Wouldn't that kill corn hip high?

"I don't know why it's so hard for John to share any information with me," I complained to Alex as I handed him a piece of cake later that night.

He took the plate. "Maybe you should bribe him with cake."

I plopped down on my couch beside him. "I mean it. He's infuriating."

He took a big bite of cake and made an *mmm* sound low in his throat. "Who said you can't cook?"

Very funny. He knew I'd gotten the coconut cake in the freezer section at Wal-Mart. All I'd had to do was thaw it out. My kind of cooking.

"While you're changing the subject with flattery, let's not forget my basketball-playing ability," I said.

He grinned. "Oh, c'mon, Miss-Used-to-

Be-a-Coach, you can play circles around me on the court, and you know it."

"Are you fishing for compliments?" I asked, laughing. "You're as good as you were in high school. And if I remember correctly, you lettered in every sport at Lake View High."

Neuro jumped up on the couch beside him, and Alex stroked her fur. Her purring vibrated the whole room.

"She's complimenting you," I said.

"She's just hoping to get a cake crumb." He ruffled her head, which she usually hated, but she pushed against his hand instead of walking away.

I took his empty plate and put it in the sink.

"Want to go sit out on the porch with a letterman?" He waggled his eyebrows.

I laughed at his silliness and pushed open the back door. We had just settled into the lawn chairs to watch Mr. Persi, my golden retriever, bounding around the fenced-in yard when the cell phone in my pocket rang.

"I'll call them back, whoever it is." I slid it out and glanced at the caller ID. "Weird. It's Bob."

Alex raised an eyebrow. "You'd better take it. If you don't, your curiosity will drive us both crazy."

Even when I was working at the club, Bob rarely called me after work hours. And since the day I quit, he hadn't called at all.

"Hey, Bob. What's up?" Mr. Persi came over and plopped down on the porch between us.

"They came and got Lisa for more questioning," Bob said with no preamble. He sounded so rattled, I wouldn't have recognized his voice if not for the caller ID. "In the police car."

"They took Lisa in? Why?" I glanced over toward Alex, who was absently patting Mr. Persi.

"The gun belongs to her." Bob's voice choked up. "It's her gun. The gun that killed J.D. Her prints were on it. On the gun. They really think she did it." His words were so jumbled, I wondered if he even realized he was repeating himself.

I didn't know what to say. Any platitude I offered would be just that. "Bob, you need to stay calm. I'm sure they'll realize she's innocent." Lisa was self-centered and totally self-absorbed, but that didn't make her a murderer. Or was she? My mind began to race. Had something happened to make Lisa want to kill J.D? Lisa always seemed to think that if she wanted something, it was hers. Maybe in this case she realized she didn't want J.D., so she eliminated him. But like I'd told Debbie, surely breaking up would be easier. And less messy.

"First she married Larry, that abusive —" His voice choked. "Now this. Hasn't she been through enough?"

"Her husband abused her?" Okay, I officially felt terrible. I'd have guessed it to be the other way around, if anything. I couldn't imagine Lisa putting up with being mistreated. But I guess that just showed that anything was possible.

"Yes. And she's finally putting it behind her." He took a shuddering breath. "Jenna, would you come over to the gym and talk to her tomorrow? That is, if they let her come home." I could hear the tears in his voice. "I need you to help me clear her name."

"I'll be there first thing in the morning, Bob. I don't go to the diner until noon."

"Thanks, Jenna. I'll make sure she's there. It means a lot to me to know you're supporting her. I know you've had your differences, but she needs all of her friends around her right now." He lowered his voice, and after years of working with him, I could easily visualize the sheepish expression on his face. "And, by the way, you know you're welcome to use the club pool anytime."

If I'd been the type to kick a man while he was down, I'd have made a sarcastic comment about selling more T-shirts that way, but I settled for, "Thanks. I'll do that."

To be honest, swimming in the lake was getting a little uncomfortable. The weather could turn nippy without warning. Yes, I'm a wimp. But I wasn't about to admit to Bob how much I was missing the perks of my old job.

"I'm glad we cleared that up." He stopped speaking to me, and I could hear a muted conversation in the background. Then, "Jenna, Wilma said Lisa just called and they're bringing her home now. I have to go."

"Okay. I'll see you tomorrow morning." I hit the END key and dropped the phone in my pocket.

I looked over at Alex. "You heard?"

He nodded.

"You know it'll kill Bob if Lisa is guilty. She's the light of his and Wilma's lives."

"Not to mention the boss of their lives. They shouldn't have spoiled her quite so much. At least that's my opinion." Alex looked up at the moonlit sky. "We won't spoil our kids like that, will we?"

"Not if we have five or six like you want

80

to. Who would have time to spoil them?" I grinned at him. "Who would have time to even take care of them?" He had been teasing me about wanting a big family. A really big family.

He leaned over and kissed me softly then pulled back and caressed my cheek with his thumb. "You know what?"

I shook my head mutely as I stared into his sparkling eyes.

"As long as you're in my family, whatever size it is will be just perfect."

Mr. Persi barked loudly and pushed between us.

Alex laughed. "At least I have his seal of approval. I'm not so sure about Neuro."

My cat had always been a tad neurotic — hence her name. But after Mr. Persi trotted into our lives and stayed, she quit pulling her fur out. And since Alex had been hanging around, she seemed more relaxed than ever. "Neuro loves you."

"And . . . ?" he teased.

"And so do I."

"I never get tired of hearing it."

Wasn't that perfect? Because I never got tired of saying it.

After Alex left, I thought about what he said about our children. We had truly come a long way since earlier in the summer when he was too busy even to think about a future with me.

When Carly called as I was getting ready for bed, I was still smiling. "Hello."

"Hi."

Her gloomy voice reminded me of the apparent fuss Mama and I had witnessed between her and Elliott earlier. "You doing okay?"

"I'm fine. I'm making a tunnel-of-fudge cake."

"For what?"

She hesitated. "Just because."

Uh-oh. Anytime Carly started baking random desserts, I knew we had a problem. "Yeah, right. So you and Elliott had a fight?"

"No." Her tone was vehement. "We just disagreed about something," she said more quietly.

"Oh," I said dryly. "Thanks for clearing that up for me."

"Enough about us. What about you? Are you getting excited about the wedding? Or has the murder sidetracked your thoughts?"

"The wedding is a means to an end. But I'm excited about Alex and me becoming a family." I stroked Neuro's thickening fur and told Carly what Alex had said earlier.

"God's really blessed us, hasn't He, Jen?"

Her words were choked with tears. I just hoped they were happy tears.

"Yes, He has."

We talked for a few more minutes, then I told her about Bob calling.

"Don't you know he's brokenhearted?" she said. "I remember how upset I was when Zac was a suspect in Hank's murder."

"Me, too," I admitted. "That's all I can think about. It's hard for me to feel an overabundance of sympathy for Lisa, but no parent should have to go through that."

"And sometimes it's hard to know where to draw the line at protecting our children from pain."

I had a strange feeling my sister wasn't talking about Bob and Lisa anymore. But I knew from experience that whatever was going on, she'd tell me when she was ready. And not a minute before.

Gail was at the desk when I arrived at the gym the next morning.

Her solemn face lit up when she saw me. "Jenna, what are you doing here?"

"I just stopped by for a few minutes." No need to tell her why I was here.

"Guess you heard about Lisa?"

I nodded. "Bob called me."

"Are you going to be here for a while? I

get a break in about thirty minutes, and we could talk."

I shook my head. "I wish I could stay. I have some things I need to ask you, but right now I have to talk to Lisa then get on to the diner." I headed toward the office, but she followed me down the hall.

"Did he give you any details?" She looked around to make sure no one could hear us.

"Not yet. I'll be back to swim as soon as I get a free minute, and we can hash everything out."

She took the hint and went back to her post. As I neared the open door to the office, I could hear Lisa talking to someone.

"They had to release me. I have an alibi."

It wasn't because I was trying to eavesdrop that I stood outside the slightly open door. It was merely that I thought it would be bad manners to barge in when she was busy with someone else. Really.

"A genuine alibi or one you conveniently set up?" a man's voice snarled.

"I told you just like I told John. Someone stole that gun. I've kept it here in the desk drawer for protection, just like you told me to."

The man's voice was low, and I couldn't hear his words.

"Larry, I don't know who else knew it was

here or who took it," Lisa said. "If I did, I'd tell the police."

"Because we both know you're so trustworthy?" the man roared.

Finally feeling guilty about eavesdropping, especially now that I realized she was talking to her husband, I reached up to tap lightly on the door. It burst open away from my fingers, and I was face-to-face with a furious man I'd never seen before. "Get out!" Lisa screamed, unnecessarily it seemed, because the man nearly bowled me over in his haste to leave. The overpowering scent of Lisa's perfume followed him out like a cloud.

I stared after him. I'd always heard that Lisa's wealthy, older husband, Lawrence Hall, favored Ricardo Montalbán during his *Fantasy Island* years. Today he looked more like the madman Ricardo played in *The Wrath of Khan.*

"Oh, it's you."

I spun around to face Lisa. "Yes, me." She sounded less than thrilled, but maybe that was more an irritated residue of the argument than it was my presence.

"What are you doing here?" she asked flatly.

Ironic. That was the very question I'd been asking myself ever since I started down the hallway to the office. "Your dad asked me to come by . . . to see if I can help you sort out your problems."

"My boyfriend was murdered, and even though Daddy always acted like you could walk on water, I'm pretty sure you can't do anything about raising the dead."

Ouch. I took a step backward. Mentally I was picturing myself saying, "Sorry, Bob. I tried."

"Other than that I only have one other problem." She glanced toward the door that Larry had just stormed out of then back at me. "Make that two. Your friend *John* thinks I'm a murderer."

"Are you?"

Her mouth dropped open. "No."

"Good. I didn't think you were."

She sat down in the office chair and stared at me.

I'd shocked her, but at least she'd stopped sniping at me for a minute. "So now that we have that out of the way, do you have any idea who might have wanted to kill J.D.?" I sat down in the chair across from the desk.

She pursed her lips and shook her head.

"I know this is hard, Lisa, but you're going to have to help me. I just have a few questions —"

She blew out her breath in disgust. "There's nothing you can ask me that the police haven't already asked. They wanted to know about my eating habits, about J.D.'s eating habits, about our relationship." She raised an eyebrow. "Personal things." She waved her little cell phone at me. "They even confiscated my phone. And questioned me about it. How long have I had it? Who's my carrier? Did I have another phone?" She sighed. "And then the big question. Why was J.D. behind the diner?"

My heartbeat picked up slightly. "What did you tell them about that?"

"I told them the truth — I have no idea. We didn't have a date or anything that night."

"Was that normal?" I sounded like a detective.

She shrugged. "Well, to tell you the truth, once he took your place here, we saw each other constantly. So we didn't go out quite as much."

I tried to keep my irritation from showing. Once he took my place. I knew she said that just to needle me. "So had you known him long? Before you started dating, I mean?"

"No. Not really." She leaned toward me. "You know how you're supposed to meet

87

guys at weddings? Well, we met him at a funeral. His grandmother's funeral. We were instantly attracted to each other."

"We who?"

"Me and J.D." She shook her head. "Good grief, Jenna. How can you solve a murder if you can't even keep up with a normal conversation?"

"I meant who was with you at the funeral? Your husband?" Maybe Lisa's ex saw the instant attraction and understandably resented it.

She snorted. "Hardly. I went with Debbie. J.D.'s grandmother and Debbie's grandmother were friends. Or something like that." She waved her hand in the air, dismissing them as unimportant. "I'm not really sure why, but Debbie thought she should go and didn't want to go by herself. So I went."

"Okay. You met him at his grandmother's funeral. And it was love at first sight. So you started dating and then hired him to work here. Right?"

"Pretty much. He decided to look for part-time work so he could stay here and get to know me better. Luckily you quit not too long after that."

I was speechless with outrage, but she didn't notice.

She dabbed at her eyes with a tissue. "Only now he's dead, and in a way it's all my fault. If he hadn't been so crazy about me, he'd have left town after the funeral." Tears rolled down her cheeks. "Because his grandma didn't leave him anything. Not a penny. And I think he was expecting to get a big inheritance. He was really disappointed."

"He wasn't rich, then?" I'd always had Lisa pegged for a girl who went where the money was.

"Well, he definitely didn't seem rich when we first started going out. He even let me buy my own dinner. If he hadn't been so good-looking I probably wouldn't have gone out with him again." She wiped her eyes once more. "But after a couple of weeks, he started paying for everything. He even took me to Tunica. And gave me money to play the slots. But of course, I didn't tell John any of that."

"Any idea where he got the money?"

"Now, how would I know that?" She rolled her eyes.

"Well, you *were* dating him." I may have sounded a little sharp. Probably.

"And that was the only reason I agreed to be fingerprinted. John told me it was to eliminate my prints so that they could find the killer." She tossed the tissue in the garbage, and her tears dried as quickly as they came. "But now he's using my fingerprints to try and prove I killed J.D. He tricked me so he would have someone to arrest," she snarled. "I can't believe I trusted him."

"Lisa, they needed your fingerprints. And he didn't trick you. How could he know your prints would be on the gun? You have to admit it makes you look suspicious."

"It was my gun, so of *course* it had my prints. It's not my fault someone stole it out of my drawer."

"How long had it been missing?"

"How should I know? I hardly ever noticed it." She shrugged. "I didn't even know it *was* missing. *You* could have taken it for all I know."

I ignored that dig, but I wanted to beat my head against the wall. Or maybe Lisa's head. Not enough to hurt her, of course, but maybe just enough to gently knock some sense into her. Yeah, right.

I couldn't believe she was talking to me like this when all I was doing was trying to help. Deep breath. "Maybe you should tell John the truth. That J.D. didn't have any money, and then all of a sudden, he did."

"And maybe you should mind your own

business."

"Lisa, what was Larry so upset about earlier?"

She narrowed her eyes. "Since when is my relationship with my husband your business?"

"I . . ." It really wasn't often that I was at a loss for words.

"Look. Thanks for stopping by, but I'll get Daddy to hire a professional. Someone who can prove that I'm innocent. Not an amateur sleuth that got lucky a couple of times." She wiggled her fingers. "So, see ya."

"Right. Well, I have to go to work now." I gritted my teeth and counted to ten as I walked out the door, taking care not to slam it.

6

Happier'n a dead pig in the sunshine

"Jenna, can you call Susan and see if she can come in today?" Carly stirred a steaming pot of soup and nodded toward the list of waitress phone numbers on the wall by the phone. "Alice called. She and Harvey won't be in, so I had to put Vini as host." She turned toward me. "I hope he can do it. Do you think he can?"

"Sure. Leading people to a table should be easier than taking orders and delivering food." I reached back to tie the apron around my waist. "Are Harvey and Alice sick?"

"Alice said John asked Harvey to come by the station and answer some questions." She dipped some of the soup into a small bowl and blew on it. "Alice sounded really upset. She said she was going with him." Carly sipped a spoonful of the liquid and frowned.

"Taste this."

"Wonder what they wanted with Harvey?" I stared at the soup. That conversation I'd overheard between Harvey and Alice the night of the murder had *not* been about soup. The question was, what *had* it been about?

"I've no idea. But I guess you're going to try and find out." Carly added some garlic powder to the pot of soup. "I don't think John will tell you."

I ignored her allusion to my curiosity and called Susan, who agreed to come in and do an earlier shift. When I hung up, I quickly got into my apron and hit the floor running.

"Welcome to Down Home Diner, ma'am." Vini's voice floated to the table where I was writing an elderly couple's order. I glanced up in time to see a flamboyantly dressed woman pat Vini's cheek.

Her voice didn't float. It trumpeted across the packed diner. "Well, sweet thing, you can welcome me anytime, anywhere."

Vini blanched, grabbed a menu, and fairly raced to an empty table in my section.

"Your waitress will be right with you." He wiped his brow and headed back to the front of the diner, making strange grimaces in my direction. I assumed he meant,

"We've got a live one here." I finished the order I was taking and excused myself.

As I walked to the table, I studied the new arrival. She was one of those people whose age isn't readily apparent, but I guessed her to be somewhere in her forties. Her jet black hair was teased within an inch of its life and piled high on her head. Her eyes were so heavily mascaraed I was surprised she could blink. More noticeable was her dress, or lack thereof. We had the standard NO SHOES, NO SHIRT, NO SERVICE sign on our door. We might need to revise that.

She had on a skirt and a top, of sorts. The white top was the scantiest of halters, and the skirt, black leather, was short enough to qualify as micro-mini. Her white boots were straight out of the sixties. Beside her brilliantly red lips was a beauty mark. A tattooed snake crawled up her right arm and coiled lovingly around her neck. As I approached the table, she gave me a cheerful grin.

"Welcome to Down Home Diner. What can I get you to drink?" I gave her my standard opening as I pulled my order pad and pencil from my pocket.

"I'll have a beer in a bottle. The best you've got. I'm celebrating."

"Sorry, ma'am. This is a dry county. We

don't serve alcoholic beverages. But we have really good sweet tea or lemonade."

"What kinda burg have I landed in?" she asked loudly. "A gal can't even get a drink?" She lowered her voice slightly. "C'mon, sweet cakes, I know you got the good stuff stashed somewheres. Just bring it in a tea glass. I won't rat you out. It ain't every day your ship comes in, but mine did, and I aim to celebrate."

"I'm really sorry. We don't have anything alcoholic on the premises. But our tea is worth celebrating. Tell you what. I'll bring you a glass on the house. If you don't like it, you won't be out anything." Carly gave away pies to police officers; surely she wouldn't mind if I gave tea to keep the peace.

"Well, the price is right. Go ahead."

As I returned with her tea, I noticed others in the café were eyeing our unusual customer with interest. She was returning the favor, meeting glances all around the room. I rattled off the specials and she ordered, but as I turned to hand the order in, she wrapped long fingers topped with pointed, blood-red nails around my wrist.

"Hang on a minute, honey. Let's talk."

"Let me turn your order in." I gingerly disengaged my wrist. "Then I'll take a break. That way I can talk without getting jumped by the boss." I was careful not to say this loud enough for anyone to hear and repeat it to Carly. I really didn't want to get jumped by my big sis. I handed the woman's order through the window to the kitchen and returned to her table. As I sat, she pulled a pack of cigarettes from the small purse she had slung around her shoulder. I must've looked as shocked as I felt, since there were NO SMOKING signs on every wall.

"What? No smoking here, either?" She shook her head as she replaced the pack. "Man. What do you people do for entertainment?"

"Well, we eat a lot," I deadpanned, and was rewarded with a loud crack of laughter.

She slapped the table with her open palm. "Girlfriend, you are a riot."

"What brings you to our little town?"

"Little is the right word. It sure wasn't to be entertained. Nope. I came on a mission. I am a woman on a pilgrimage, you might say. This little one-horse town is where one of my old mistakes came right. Did that ever happen to you?" She nudged me.

"I don't know." I was confused, and it showed.

"Well, I'll tell ya, sister, I've made plenty

of mistakes in my life. I ain't ashamed to say it. But one of my first ones was marrying a weasel. Have you ever done that? You married?"

The kitchen window bell rang. "Not yet." I walked over to pick up her order then set the full plate in front of her. She continued to talk as I sat back down

"Well, take my advice and steer shy of it. And if you do get married, make sure he ain't a weasel. My man, Jimmy, he was slick. And sweet-talking? Why, that man could talk the bark off a tree." She paused to take a gulp of tea. "This tea's good. Anyhow, he was crooked as a snake. See this snake on my shoulder? I got that after Jimmy and me split up. That's my reminder not to fall for any more snakes. Yeah, me and Jimmy got married when I was just a girl. Then I found out he wadn't what you might call honest. No sirree." She took a large bite of mashed potatoes and gravy and kept talking as she chewed. "But we did one thing right. We made wills. You got a will?"

"Yes, ma'am."

"Smart girl. Yep. Me and Jimmy made wills and left all our worldly possessions — don't that sound fine? — all our worldly possessions to each other. I never thought much about it until a lawyer called me a couple days ago. He told me Jimmy had done cashed in his chips in a little one-horse town nobody'd ever heard of. And I'm thirty thousand dollars richer. Best thing Jimmy Dean Finley ever done for me was die."

"You mean — ? J. D. Finley was your husband?"

"Ex, honey. I divorced him for reasons we needn't go into, over twenty years ago. But he never changed his will. So I came here on this pilgrimage to see where he bit the dust. And to celebrate."

A loud clatter jerked my eyes to the kitchen area. Debbie stood in the midst of breakage, and I noted absently that her customer must've ordered strawberry short-cake. She looked as if she had been in a wreck, splashed with strawberry juice to her knees.

"I'm sure glad that little lady wadn't bringing my food." My companion winked at me. "I b'lieve you guys need to invest in some superglue for her. Stick that tray to her hands."

"Excuse me a second," I murmured and rushed to help Debbie and Vini clean up the mess. Only Debbie didn't stick around. She simply turned and walked to the kitchen. But not before I saw the tears streaming down her face. Either Carly was going to have to find out what was bugging Debbie or buy unbreakable dishes. After we cleaned everything up, I went back to the table.

"Ain't you Mr. Clean? With hair, of course," she remarked sardonically. "That little gal needs to find herself another job. She ain't cut out for waitressing. I oughta know. I been one my own self. Along with lots of other things." A loud bark of laughter followed. "What time do you get offa work, missy?"

"Me?" My mind was blank — or numb.

"Yes, you." She snapped her fingers in my face. "Hello? You do work here, don't you?"

"Oh. Yes." I glanced at my watch. "In about twenty minutes."

"Why don't I wait for you outside under one of them big shade trees? I need somebody to show me around town, and I don't know a soul here. Unless you count poor ole Jimmy's, and that ain't much help." Another roar of laughter.

I debated. A little of this woman went a long way. On the other hand, she'd known J.D. in his youth. Perhaps she could shed some light on who would kill him, or at least why.

"I'll meet you in the parking lot in a few

minutes," I answered.

"Good girl." She left a five-dollar bill on the table and gave me a wink. "That's to celebrate my good fortune. I believe in spreading it around."

As she exited, followed by many fascinated gazes, I went to the kitchen to see if Carly needed help in view of Debbie's departure. To my surprise, Debbie, scrubbed clean of strawberries, though still somewhat stained, was dishing up food, keeping her eyes fixed on her work. I went back to waiting tables until the noon surge had subsided then hung up my apron.

I stepped into the kitchen and quickly filled Carly in on my new acquaintance.

"You're going for a ride with a stranger?" she asked, obviously puzzled.

I shrugged. "You'd just have to meet her. I need to find out as much as I can about J.D., and I think she can help me."

"Keep your cell phone on."

"I will," I called and headed out to meet my new acquaintance.

"I was about to come hunting you, honey. But I figured you couldn't get past me unless you went out the back door and hid behind the Dumpster." I shivered. The Dumpster was the last place I would ever hide from anyone.

"Hop in this roadster of mine, and let's see what this little burg has to offer." She opened the passenger door of an older Mustang, fire-engine red and well kept. I climbed in, and she ran around and sank into the driver's seat, turned the key, and revved the engine. I glanced around. All I needed was for John or Seth to run up and write a ticket. I'd never live it down. But we got safely away in a spurt of loose gravel and headed down the main drag of Lake View.

"We get lots of tourists, Mrs. Finley," I began.

She began to look around, even craning her neck to look in the backseat. I clung to the seat belt strap with white knuckles as the car careened from one lane to the other.

She brayed another of her loud laughs.

"What are you doing?" I asked.

"I was looking for Mrs. Finley. If you meant me, my name's Jolene. I ain't been 'Mrs.' nothin' since I was a kid. And I took my maiden name after Jimmy Dean left me. Yep, Jolene Highwater, that's me. Now, little lady, what's your name?"

"Jenna Stafford." I waited a beat, although I doubted Jolene would be the type to watch the Olympics, much less remember one has-been from years ago. Apparently I was right.

101

"Pleased to meetcha, honey." She removed her right hand from the steering wheel and stuck it out. I shook it and released it quickly, hoping she'd return it and her attention to where they belonged. She noticed my nervousness and laughed again. She certainly was a happy woman. "Jimmy always said I was the worst kinda driver, a polite one. When I talk to someone, I look at 'em."

"Well, we have several hills and curves in this part of the country, so that may not be a good idea." I spoke quickly, lest she look too long and miss a curve.

"You know, I hadn't even hardly thought about Jimmy Dean for the last few years. I'd really put him out of my mind. He was just a youthful mistake, you know?" She looked over at me, and I nodded.

After what seemed like an eternity, she looked back at the road. "But ever since that lawyer guy called, I keep remembering when we was together. I thought there wadn't no good memories, but now most of 'em seem good. Ain't it funny how our minds can play tricks on us?"

It was. My mind was tricking me into believing that if we didn't stop while we talked, somebody might be cashing in on *my* will. "There's a scenic overlook up here on your left that's really beautiful." I crossed my fingers that she'd pull in.

She obligingly whipped the little car in and killed the motor. We got out and looked across mountains faintly colored with fall leaves. My legs still trembled a little, but I walked over and sat down, willing myself to relax.

In front of us, mountain after mountain fell away until they faded into blueness. I never tired of looking at the majestic beauty of this scene. Jolene stared at it a long time without speaking. Almost a miracle. Then she slowly lit a cigarette and took a long drag.

She loosed a stream of smoke and looked at me. "I'd like to ask you a favor." She spoke soberly. "I know we just met, and you don't owe me a thing. But I'm kinda in what you might call a pickle. Turns out I'm the executor of Jimmy's will. He hadn't got no close kin left. So I have to decide how to dispose of the body when they get done with it and release it." She stared out at the mountains then back at me. "I thought I'd just have him cremated and get on back to my life, but now that I'm here, I don't think I can do that."

I wondered again about Jimmy Dean Finley. What kind of life must he have lived to have no one who wanted to plan a funeral for him? "You know, his grandma lived here. She died a little while back. He came to the funeral and just stayed on."

"Yeah? Her and him never did get along when I knew him. But I guess, like they say, blood's thicker'n water. You think I oughta have him buried here?"

"There were folks in town who were quite fond of him," I said carefully. "They might get a sense of closure if you have a funeral."

She snorted. "Closure? Reckon that's why someone killed him? So they could get closure?"

"Do you know why someone might have killed him?"

She threw her cigarette down and ground it into the dirt with her heel. Then she carefully picked up the butt and stuck it into her pocket. "I have no idea. Unless Jimmy changed quite a lot, it coulda been just about anything. Wonder how much a funeral would cost? I could spend a thousand or so of what I'm getting, I guess. After all, if it wadn't for him, I wouldn't have any."

"I could show you where the local funeral home is."

"Tell ya what — you do that later on. Right now I'm ready to find the nearest watering hole. I've had about as much of this dry-county stuff as I can handle for one day."

We climbed into the Mustang, and the engine roared to life. She spun gravel as she peeled onto the road and headed back to town.

The next night, Carly walked into the deserted dining room as I was wiping the crumbs from the last dirty table. "Think you and I can handle the cleanup if I let the others go on home?"

"Sure." We hadn't had a chance to talk since the diner opened. I followed her into the kitchen.

Debbie and Susan both looked relieved when Carly told them their shifts were officially over.

Susan picked up her purse. "I'm dog tired. I'd forgotten how hard this was." She must have noticed Carly's funny look, because she quickly clarified, "I'm thrilled to have the job. It's just been several years since I've waitressed. I'll have to get back in the groove."

"You're doing great," Carly assured her. "Thanks for pulling a double yesterday."

"See y'all tomorrow." Debbie followed Susan out the door. "I'm going home to put my feet up."

Carly and I finished putting the dishes away. Together we walked out to do a last-minute check of the dining room before tackling the bathrooms.

Vini was standing near the front door.

"Vini!" Carly said. "I thought you were already gone."

"No. Is there anything else I can do? I will be happy to put the dishes away or sweep." Dark circles under his eyes made him look exhausted.

Carly and I exchanged glances. "Um, Vini, I told you your shift was over. Why don't you go on home now and get some sleep?" Carly smiled at the waiter. "I appreciate your willingness to work, but we're almost finished."

"Okay. If you are sure there isn't anything I can do." In spite of his agreeable words, he didn't move. "I just wanted to help out. I really appreciate you giving me this job."

"You do a great job. Harvey says lots of people ask to be seated in your section."

"I do my best." He smiled modestly. "I make good tips, too. I think a lot of people just like to hear me talk."

His accent did stand out in our little Southern town. Not to mention his European charm and Italian good looks. And according to Harvey, older women, especially, liked to sit in his section. Maybe because he had the courtliness of an old-fashioned gentleman.

"Well, we have to finish cleaning up, hon." Carly made a shooing motion at him. "You probably need to go on home and study."

"Yeah, I get to clean the restrooms." I pulled latex gloves out of my pocket. "I can't wait."

"Would you like me to help? I can do the men's room." He picked up a pair of gloves.

I glanced at Carly. She must have read my mind. There were some gift horses you didn't refuse. An offer to clean the men's room definitely fell in that category. "Sure. You can if you don't mind." She handed him an apron. With the extra help, it didn't take but a few minutes to finish up the cleaning and put the supplies away. As we gathered up our personal things, Carly stepped back and looked at Vini's face. "Are you getting enough sleep?"

"Between studying and working here, I don't sleep a lot. But I rest plenty." He pulled off his latex gloves. "I need to work all the hours you will let me have so I can make enough to pay for school." He tossed his apron into the laundry hamper. "And I have to maintain good grades, so I have to study a great deal, too."

107

"Wow, you do have a full schedule. Not much time for a social life, I suppose." Carly smiled at him.

"Social life? What is that?" He grimaced. "The only females I see are right here at the diner. Remember the woman with the snake tattoo?"

I smiled as I thought of Jolene.

"Hiding from her. That is my idea of a social life."

"You need to get out more, honey," Carly said as she carefully locked the front door.

We walked out onto the back porch. Carly locked it, too. We all started out to the vehicles together. Vini veered off toward his old van.

Carly looked at me. "I forgot I parked around front."

I motioned toward my car a few feet away. "I'll give you a ride around there. It's safer that way."

She climbed into the passenger seat, and I started the car.

"Poor Vini. He looked so exhausted tonight. Kind of overwhelmed." My tender-hearted sister sounded distressed.

"Well, no wonder with his busy schedule. I don't think I could face going to school and studying plus working here as many hours as he does." I put the car in reverse and slowly drove around the building.

Carly sighed. "Yeah, and he looked worried, too. I guess he really needs the money."

A sudden memory of Vini standing by the cash register when we'd walked into the dining room an hour earlier flashed through my mind. "You don't think he needed it bad enough to kill J.D. and rob him, do you?" I dismissed the idea as soon as the words came out of my mouth.

Carly shook her head. "No way do I think that sweet boy would even think about such a thing."

"Me either. But you know Mama always told us some people would do anything for money."

"True. But I don't think Vini falls into that category. Do you?" She glanced at me as I pulled up beside her car. "Besides, I hadn't heard J.D. was robbed. Was he?"

"No idea. If he was, that bit of gossip hasn't hit the streets yet." I wondered if I could pry that information out of John with a free piece of pie. Probably not.

Carly turned toward me. "Not to change the subject or anything, but I hope you have a good time tomorrow." She leaned back in her seat. "Are you nervous about spending the day with the 'in-laws to be'?"

I shook my head. Then I nodded. Then I

shrugged. Talk about mixed signals. "I don't know. You know I always loved Alex's parents even when we were kids. I guess I'm afraid our engagement will change things some." I turned off the motor. "But having premium seats at a Cardinals game will be worth overcoming my nerves." I grinned at Carly.

"I'm sure they knew that, too." She climbed into her car. "Have a good time. Call me when you get home."

"I will, but it'll be really late. Don't work too hard without me." As I pulled out of the parking lot, I realized that Carly and I hadn't ended up getting to talk alone after all. Pretty soon we'd just have to sit down and visit.

Dear Pru,

I've been married three months to the man of my dreams. Our marriage couldn't be better. Except for one minor detail. His parents hate me. They tell him they like me, but I know they don't. They're not rude, but if you could see how stilted they act when I'm with them, you'd know they can't stand to be around me. I really don't know what to do.

More Outlaw Than In-law

Dear Outlaw,

Be patient. Chances are that if you find a common interest and work to get to know his parents better, they'll like you. And even though I know you can't see it, some reserve could be normal for them. Sometimes our imaginations wreak havoc in our lives. Be sure paranoia isn't part of your problem.

7

Everything is lovely and
the goose hangs high.

When Alex rang the bell, it was morning but still dark outside. I yanked the door open and pulled him inside. "I need your help."

"Whoa, water girl. What's wrong?"

"Is this shirt okay?"

He looked at my red Cardinals shirt then back up at my face. "Is this a trick question?"

"No!"

"Of course it's fine."

"Just fine?"

"Perfect. As usual," he said with a slightly uncertain smile.

I stared in the foyer mirror at my wild curls. "Why did I leave my hair down? Everybody knows you wear a ponytail to a baseball game." I swooped my hair up and secured it.

"Uh-oh," Alex said.

I turned to him. "Uh-oh *what?*"

"Uh-oh, I didn't get the ponytail memo."

I smacked his arm. "Very funny."

He held up a bag. "But I did bring you something that actually goes with that hairstyle."

I opened the bag and pulled out two red caps emblazoned with the team logo. "Thanks." I froze with it halfway to my hair. "You don't think it's too much for us to be matching?"

He placed his own cap on his head. "Too much?"

"Too . . . like we're shoving our engagement in your parents' face?"

He laughed then stopped when he saw my face. "Honey, let's sit down and talk about whatever's got you so frantic."

"We can't sit down. If we're late, we might miss the beginning of the ball game." Or worse, cause his parents to miss it. I'd looked on the Internet after Alex told me about their engagement gift to us. I felt sure they'd had to pay at least a hundred dollars each for four tickets right behind home plate.

Neuro and Mr. Persi paced around me as if they knew my happy ending was about to explode into a million pieces. I gave them each a pat. "We'll be back late tonight, guys. Zac will be by a few times to visit. Be good and take care of each other."

Alex escorted me onto the porch then put one hand on my back as we walked to the truck. He helped me in and shut the door. I think by now he wasn't sure I wouldn't run.

We didn't speak until we were leaving Lake View, and he glanced over at me. "Want to tell me what that was all about back there?"

"What?" I stared out the passenger window at the trees and pastures flying by.

"The meltdown."

"Just because I had a hard time deciding what to wear? That represents a meltdown?" I joked. "Remind me never to take you shopping with me."

"Fine," he said, a slight frown crossing his face. "Obviously, we're going to spend a four-hour drive pretending that nothing's wrong."

I forced my shoulders to relax and blew out the breath I hadn't realized I'd been holding. "I'm a little nervous about seeing your parents."

"You saw them when they came through town a few weeks ago," he pointed out in a reasonable tone.

"Yes, but then I was just your girlfriend, and they were in town about an hour. This is going to be an all-day thing, including going to their house after the game." I cut my gaze over to him. "And now we're engaged."

He shook his head and tapped his hand on the steering wheel. "Which my parents are thrilled about."

I snorted. "Of course that's what they're going to tell you."

He drove for a minute then sighed. "You want to know the truth? If I married anyone else, they'd be disappointed."

I opened my mouth, and he held up his hand.

"And no, that's not why I'm marrying you."

I sighed. He knew me too well. But he'd calmed my nerves. For now, anyway.

"He's out of there," Coach Campbell roared.

The Cincinnati batter didn't move out of the box, and Alex's dad threw out his hands in disgust. "What was that?"

Demaree patted her husband's arm. "Honey, just because we have seats behind home plate doesn't mean you're the ump."

"Maybe I should be," he grumbled, but

115

his grin gave him away. He leaned forward and looked across his wife at me. "What do you think, Jenna? Was I right or wrong?"

Alex cleared his throat. "Now, Dad. Jenna —"

While Alex was trying to protect me, St. Louis's pitcher wound up for another pitch and released it. The umpire called strike three, and the inning was over.

I laughed and interrupted. "Coach, I think you were absolutely right. He's out of there."

"You always were a wise one," he said.

Yeah, like when I was wise enough to know my swimming career was all washed up. I pushed the negative thought away and scolded myself like Carly and I always did when the kids got a little self-centered. *It's not all about you,* I reminded myself.

Demaree slipped her hand in mine and gave it a small squeeze. She leaned over and spoke softly in my ear. "Forgive our enthusiasm, Jenna. We're so happy that you and Alex are going to be married. I'm afraid we're a little giddy."

"Are you sure?" I blurted out.

Puzzlement crossed her face. "Of course I'm sure. Why would you ask that?"

I shrugged. "No reason, I guess. I know I let Coach down when I lost the Olympics."

Her pretty face grew stern. "Let him down?" she said, no longer lowering her voice. She flashed a look at her husband. "Mike, Jenna thinks she let you down by losing in the Olympics."

His eyes widened with surprise, and either he missed his calling as an actor, or his shock was genuine. "How did you let me down? You were the best swimmer I ever coached. You did everything I asked of you, even when you thought you couldn't. You were a joy to coach, Jenna."

I resisted the urge to go into it further. Now was neither the time nor the place as the first Cardinal batter approached the batter's box. "Never mind," I said, smiling. "Thank you."

By the time the Cards won a rowdy victory, I'd almost managed to stop thinking of Alex's parents as my ex-coach and his wife. If they could get over my early failure and the impact it no doubt had on their lives, surely I could, too. I was a grown woman, after all.

But when we got to his parents' house after the game, all my earlier nervousness returned with a vengeance. I climbed down from the truck. "Whoa, it's beautiful," I said to Alex, as we approached the white two-story house with its bright green roof. "I especially love the front porch and the swing." His folks came out just as I finished speaking. They'd left the ball game only a few minutes before us, but when Alex called them ten minutes ago to tell them we were stopped for road construction, they were already home. One of the joys of being a local and knowing all the shortcuts.

They accepted my compliments and ushered us into the house. We bypassed the formal living room and went straight to the family room, a comfortable area with overstuffed chairs and a fireplace.

And walls and shelves covered with pictures. I noticed one of Alex as I remembered him from childhood. He was so cute, even then. I followed his pictorial progress from infancy to adulthood. All those moments I'd missed. There he was at bat in a baseball game; here he was shooting a long shot on the basketball court. There were pictures of him swimming, camping, graduating college. Holding up his shingle. There were several of him in groups, both formal and informal. None with him and a girl alone. I wondered if his parents wished he'd married someone from his college days instead of the girl who choked under pressure.

"Hey, water girl," Alex said from near my shoulder. "Your wall's over here."

I glanced at him in puzzlement as he turned me to face the wall across the room. Photos of Coach Mike and his pupils. I walked across for a closer look. To my surprise, I was in more than half the photos.

"My star student," Coach said from behind us.

I spun around. "Up to a point."

He chuckled. "Up to the point that Super Girl finally showed she was human by getting sick at the worst possible time? But even then you were the best I ever coached."

I ignored the last part of his comment as politeness and focused on the first part. "You didn't think my illness was just nerves? A way to wimp out?" Until I said it aloud, I hadn't realized that deep down that was what I'd feared all these years.

"Nerves?" he boomed. "Nerves don't cause a 102-degree fever. You had no business competing. If you'll remember, I told you to withdraw, and you refused. And I felt it had to be your decision, since you'd trained so long and hard. Your parents reluctantly agreed with me. But your body couldn't fight infection and win a gold medal at the same time."

"Or any medal," I reminded him just in case he'd forgotten.

Demaree slipped her arm around me and

gave me a side hug. "Girl, you qualified for the Olympics. Where's the shame in that? Even if you hadn't been sick, which you definitely were, there are only so many medals. But being there was a victory. You're an amazing swimmer." She walked over and took her husband's hand. "And even more important, in our eyes, you're an amazing person. So don't identify yourself by what you can *do,* but by who you are. You're a beautiful, caring Christian woman who has had some disappointments. But from those disappointments has come determination and strength of character. And we're proud to have you for our daughter-in-law."

I reached up to wipe a tear, and Alex grasped my wrist lightly.

"What a sneaky way of showing off your engagement ring," he said and held up my hand. What a sneaky way of changing the subject.

I loved him.

And his parents.

When we pulled into my driveway that night, I wondered for the hundredth time why I'd been so nervous about seeing his parents again.

Alex got out and walked me to the door. "Want me to come in and make sure everything's okay?"

"I'm sure everything's fine." I glanced at my watch. "Zac was here just a couple of hours ago to let Mr. Persi out."

It was a little before ten. Not too late to give Carly a call. When I got inside, I did, and she answered on the first ring. "I was hoping you'd call. How'd it go?"

I hit the speakerphone button and laid the phone on the vanity. "Great. I had a wonderful time." I slid the ponytail holder from my hair and picked up my brush. "They were so nice to me."

"All that worrying for nothing," Carly teased.

"I guess you're right. You know what?" I ran the brush through my tangled hair. "They're really happy we're engaged."

"Of course they are. They know a good thing when they see it." I could hear the smile in her voice.

"And so do I. I'm so glad Alex and I finally worked things out." I looked at myself in the mirror. Even I could see that I looked happy. "Now if I can just get you and Elliott all fixed up." I teased her.

"You know how mom always tells you to mind your own business?" She laughed. "Well, never mind. That dog won't hunt."

"I guess you're implying that I'm nosy?"

Nothing new there.

"Well, if the shoe fits." She laughed. "And we know it's exactly your size. And you have the mate in your closet."

"Okay, silly. But you'd tell me if there was anything I could do to help y'all, right?" I laid the brush down.

"Of course." She lowered her voice. "I'm just not going to rush into anything."

I hardly considered a year "rushing," but Carly would do things in her own time. Harvey was right when he said she had a mind of her own.

"By the way," I said. "Larry was at the club when I went to see Lisa. He didn't seem too happy."

"Lisa's husband? I don't imagine knowing Lisa was seeing J.D. made him happy."

"Well, the thing is, he knew exactly where she kept the gun. In fact, he's the one who told her to bring it to the club and put it in the drawer."

"Did she tell you that?"

And even though she couldn't see me, I blushed. "No, I overheard it when I was standing outside her office."

"Who, you? Nosy? What was I thinking? Eavesdropping, huh?" Carly said dryly.

"No, in this instance I was just waiting politely until she was free to see me," I said piously. "The point is, Larry knew about the murder weapon and where it was.

"Hmm . . ." Carly said. "You know what?"

"What?"

"Didn't you tell me before you quit that Lisa was laying it on thick to some of the members about the club being safe because she had a gun and knew how to use it?"

I slapped my forehead with my free hand. "Carly, you're right. I can't believe I forgot that. But she was bragging to a bunch of guys one morning when I came in."

"So a lot of people knew about the gun. It wouldn't take a rocket scientist to find it in her desk drawer."

"That's true. But Bob specifically said Larry was abusive. And if he was jealous . . ."

"Yeah," Carly said. "We know firsthand that jealousy can lead to murder."

"Oh well, I may find out more tomorrow. I'm going to swim at the club in the morning."

"So you and Bob made up?"

"I guess. To an extent."

"If it's not war, it's peace," she said. "Be thankful for it."

"Believe me, I am."

It felt weird but totally natural to be back at

the club pool for my morning swim. I had spent so much time here that not coming for the last few weeks had felt strange. I shook off introspections and focused on getting my laps in. No use crying over spilled milk. Or in this case, chlorinated water. Definitely better than the lake. And so nice to have it to myself. Or so I thought.

"Hey! They let just anybody in here?"

I set a new record for going from a breast-stroke to a high jump in seven feet of water. Which Seth thought was hilarious.

"What are you doing here so early?" I excused myself for sounding like a petulant child on the basis of extreme surprise.

"I heard the great Jenna Stafford was working out here again, and I had to come check it out." A grin still marked his features, so at least my rudeness hadn't been too obvious. "Just kidding. Passing by on my way to the weight room. I'll be back later in case you need company." With a jaunty salute, he left, but before I could soak in the solitude, Amelia came in. So much for a quiet swim.

Amelia motioned imperiously.

Like a puppet on strings, I obediently swam to the edge of the pool.

She handed me a towel. "Put this around you and sit with me a minute." She proceeded to a corner table and made herself comfortable.

I followed. Like I had a choice. As I draped the towel over me for maximum coverage and warmth, Amelia looked around suspiciously then leaned forward and put a finger to her lips. Apparently she was channeling James Bond. I glanced around nervously. Were enemy agents about to descend? Was the room bugged? Was Amelia slightly batty?

"What's wrong, Amelia?" I apparently hadn't quite banished my inner pouty child.

"Shh. I don't want anyone to see us talking." She got up and looked out the steamy windows of the pool room doors. Satisfied that we weren't being observed, she resumed her seat. "Remember what I asked you to do for me?"

Oops. I was drawing a blank. "What?"

She pursed her lips and shook her head as if she felt sorry for me for having such a low IQ. "You were going to ask around about Ricky."

"Oh yes. That. Well . . ." Pause for throat clearing and brain searching. "So far, not much." I'd been a little busy trying to help Bob keep Lisa out of jail and find out who really killed J.D. But since Amelia knew I wasn't directly involved with this murder investigation, I knew she'd never buy that as an excuse. And considering that this very moment, Ricky's partner was in the weight room next door, I could make up for lost time. "I've got a plan, though."

"Plans are only as efficient as the planner," she said primly.

I pushed a wet strand of hair off my face and stared at her. Was she insulting me?

Her expression lightened a little. I think she realized she'd almost pushed the "favor" envelope too far. "Please hurry. Tiffany's pushing like mad for me to get this wedding planned."

"Okay, I'll get back to you as soon as I find out anything."

She gave me a terse nod and stood, then with a surreptitious wave of dismissal, sauntered out. I wanted to call out a witty "We've got to stop meeting like this," but I felt sure she wouldn't appreciate it. So I stood and sidled toward the shower room. Even though I loved to swim, I hated getting back in the water after I'd been out for a while.

I rushed through my shower and emerged just as Seth left the men's shower room. How convenient.

He shot me a cocky grin as if I'd set up this meeting on purpose. And even if he was close to right, it definitely wasn't for the reason he was obviously hoping it was for. "Hey, babe, we've got to stop meeting like this," he drawled.

I cringed, glad I hadn't said something similar to Amelia. That old line wasn't as witty as I'd thought it might be when it was said aloud. "Hi, Seth. Did you have a good workout?"

He flexed his muscles beneath his white T-shirt. "Always."

Even for Amelia, I draw the line at admiring another man's pecs. I glanced toward the pool. "Do you swim?"

He nodded. "Like a pro." He apparently remembered who he was talking to, because he said, "Well, I may not be the best in the world." He laughed. "But at least I can swim. Ol' Rick can't swim a lick."

Talk about opportunity knocking. "He can't?"

"Nah, he always says if God intended us to swim, he'd have given us fins."

Mission accomplished. Now anyone with a brain could see that Ricky wasn't suitable for Tiffany. Imagine anyone not swimming. I smiled at my silly thoughts. "Speaking of Ricky, is he an all-right guy?"

Seth frowned at me and stumbled a little. "Yeah, he's okay. Why?"

I waved my hand airily. "I just don't know him that well . . . and now that he's playing b-ball with us on Sunday afternoons, I thought I should know a little about him."

"Like what?" Seth's face darkened.

Unsure whether to abort my mission or keep trying, I forged on. "Oh, I don't know. Like did he move here to take the police job, or was he already here when the opening came?"

"I don't know. I think he had been here a little while when the opening came up. Why?" His eyes were filled with suspicion.

"I told you. I just like to know about people. And I figured you're his best friend, since y'all are partners and all."

He shrugged. "I don't know about best friend. That sounds kinda girly. He's a pal. We don't hang out much, since he and Tiffany have a thing going on." He sent a searching look my way. "You do know about that, don't you?"

"Sure. I saw them at the cabins the other day, remember? Have they dated long? Did he date around when he first came?"

Seth's grin slipped slightly. "Why? You want to take him away from her? Did you forget that big rock on your finger?"

My eyebrows rose. "No!"

He put his hand on my arm and gazed

into my eyes. "You've made it plain to me you're engaged, and I'm dealing with that. So why are you asking about other men?"

Eek. I hadn't taken into account that he might be jealous. "Seth . . . I —"

He held up his hand. "I know. You only like me as a friend. But Tiffany's a real sweet girl. And she doesn't need you messing things up for her. So just remember, Rick's taken." He stomped off before I could assure him that I wasn't after Tiffany's boyfriend.

I knew one thing for sure. I'd never ask Amelia for another favor.

Her paybacks were too steep.

8

Between a rock and a hard place

The next night, I walked out of the diner and glanced at the digital numbers on the front of my cell phone. Only 8:30. I still had plenty of time to run by the *Monitor* and pick up some Dear Pru letters. I drove the short distance, pulled into the empty parking lot, and killed the motor.

I dreaded going in to an empty office. But picking up the letters after everyone was gone was the only way to preserve my secret identity. Even though Marge had always told me just to tell people I did some part-time work for the newspaper, she also said not to be specific about what the part-time work entailed.

So I'd gotten used to letting myself in the back door with the key Marge had given me and finding my way through the darkened offices to the desk where my letters were kept. Still, every time I unlocked this door, I thought about Hank Templeton, the former editor. And about his murder. Tonight, as I headed down the hall, I noticed a light shining under the door of the editor's office.

I shivered. Had Hank left the light on for me?

Since I didn't believe in ghosts, I hefted my carryall, wondering how much impact it would have on a skull. Not much, since I'd emptied it before I left home. I glanced around the hall. Unless I intended to yank a picture off the wall and beat the intruder over the head, I had few options. I turned to look for a more conventional weapon and tripped over a trash can.

The office door opened.

"Freeze! I've got a gun and I know how to use it," a woman's voice snarled.

"Don't shoot!" I threw my arms over my head.

"Jenna?"

"Tiffany? Thank goodness. You scared me to death."

"Yeah? Well, my heart's beating a little fast, too."

"Do you really have a gun?" I couldn't resist asking.

"Sort of." She sheepishly extended her

hand, with the index finger pointed outward and the others curled in.

"I'll have to remember that next time I get in a tight spot." I grinned. "I just came to pick up some Dear Pru letters."

"I thought you came on Tuesdays."

"I had a late date last night, and you know I can't come during business hours. There wasn't a car in the parking lot."

She motioned to her sweat suit. "Ricky's on duty tonight, and I was just out for a walk. Thought I'd stop by and catch up on some work."

I nodded. "I should've called you. Sorry."

"That's okay. Neither of us had a heart attack, so no harm done. Come on in, and let's get some letters."

As we walked down the hall, she said, "Aunt Marge says the Dear Pru column has soared in popularity since you took it over."

"Thanks. I wasn't sure at first if I could do it, but with Carly's help, and Mama's, too, actually, I —"

Tiffany stopped and frowned. "I didn't know your mom knew about you being Dear Pru."

I laughed as I walked on into the office. "She has no idea. But Mama has given us so much good advice over the years that with almost every Dear Pru letter, I remember a nugget of her wisdom to help me answer." I pulled a manila envelope stuffed full of letters out of the filing cabinet.

"Lucky you." She stepped inside the office. "I guess I was born a rebel. I've never been good at taking my mother's advice." She laughed. "Just ask her." She sat down in the chair near the desk. "Although, you may have gathered that from the other day at the diner."

"Well . . ." I wanted to be diplomatic, not my best talent. "I did get the impression she wanted you to spend more time planning your wedding." I took several letters off the stack and sat down in the chair beside Tiffany.

"She wants it to be the social event of the season." She shrugged. "Not me. If it weren't for Daddy, I'd just elope. What about you? Have you and Alex set a date yet?"

"We're planning on right around Christmas." I glanced down at my engagement ring.

She raised her eyebrows. "Don't tell my mother you're getting married that soon, or she'll be planning your wedding. Or wait . . . Do tell her, and maybe it'll get her off my case."

"I could probably use a wedding planner."

Although truthfully, I agreed with Tiffany. I didn't need a big social event to be married. Our wedding would be quiet and simple. But just as legal and romantic as a bigger one.

"Jenna?" Tiffany's normally confident voice was hesitant. "I've noticed how well you deal with my mother."

Shocked, I bit back a protest. Amelia and I dealt as well as a snake and a frog, with me being the frog. I always feared she might swallow me whole.

Tiffany continued, oblivious to my amazement. "You know, I was always a disappointment to her. She's so perfect, and I could never live up to that."

"Well . . ." I cleared my throat. "Everyone's idea of perfection is different. And a child's perception of her mother sometimes differs from the way others see her."

"How did you see your mother?"

I thought of my mom playing kickball with us when we were little, taking me to the pool, sitting patiently and proudly through endless swim meets, serving as room mother throughout my elementary years, teaching me to pray, admonishing me to pay attention to the preacher. My mom was my cheerleader, my spiritual adviser, my support. My hero.

"Well . . ." I hedged. "My mom's not your average mom. She's more like Super Mom."

"You know, when I came home on holidays, I'd see you and your sister at church with your folks, and I fantasized about being you."

"You're kidding. Why?"

She shrugged and looked a little embarrassed. "You got to live at home all the time. You weren't considered a nuisance who had to be sent to boarding school."

I shook my head. "I'm sure that's not why they sent you to boarding school. It's just that they wanted the very best for you because they loved you so much."

"Is that what you think?" She shot me a pitying look, but I thought there was a hint of hope, as well. "They had an odd way of showing it, didn't they? Actually, Daddy would've let me stay home, but Mother talked him out of it."

"Are you sure?"

She nodded. "Positive. When I was little, it was okay. I wasn't your typical cute toddler, but I was reasonably intelligent. But when I was about six, I hit a growth spurt and gained weight. From then on, I was an embarrassment to Mother. By the time I was a teenager, my weight problem had grown worse and was complicated by that common teen horror, acne. I spent several summers abroad with a nanny. Does that sound like my mother loved me?"

"Teenage years are hard for everyone," I answered, remembering the turmoil surrounding my parents and Carly. "Sometimes the best thing we can do about them is forgive and forget."

Tiffany ran her hand through her frizzy hair. "It's not like I haven't tried. A long time ago, I decided the best way to deal with her is to be myself, only more so. Hence, no makeup, no fancy clothes, no beauty salons. It kills her. And I'll let you in on a little secret. I have a whole closet full of other clothes. When I go out of town, I dress and act like everyone else. I'll never be beautiful like my mother, but I'm passable."

"Has Ricky seen you in your other guise?" I had to ask.

She laughed. "Oh yes. On a few special occasions, I've pulled out my wardrobe stash and gotten fixed up before we've gone out. Only when we were going out of town, of course. I've been to Dallas on business several times since we've been dating. A couple of times he let me get him a plane ticket and hotel room, though he wouldn't stay at the fancy hotel I stayed at. He didn't want to waste my money. And of course, we couldn't travel down together. I don't want Mother to have a heart attack, after all."

"That's nice of you," I said dryly.

She smirked. "Anyway, I promised Ricky that when we get married, I'll stop my little prank. But for now, he thinks it's a good joke on Mother, too."

"You and Ricky must have the same sense of humor," I commented. "Being able to laugh together is a good thing."

"Yes." She frowned faintly. "Though sometimes he is a little flippant about things I feel are important." She hurriedly added, "Not that I'm criticizing him."

"Nobody's perfect," I answered. I could almost feel Amelia at my elbow, urging me on. "Where did you and Ricky meet?"

She rolled her eyes. "That's a crazy story. I hadn't been back in town long, and Mother insisted on buying me a new car. Of course, the little hybrid I wanted wasn't good enough for her daughter, so she got me a gas-guzzling Hummer. Can you believe it? Anyhow, I was cruising through town when blue lights came on behind me. I pulled over to let the officer chase down whatever dangerous criminal he was after, but it was me. Ricky had just joined the force and didn't realize who I was."

I noted that she was as arrogant as Amelia,

though in a nicer way.

"When I told him my name, he asked if I was any relation to the mayor. We had a good laugh when he discovered he'd pulled the mayor's daughter over for speeding."

"You drive a Hummer?" I asked, remembering the little Toyota Prius she'd been driving the day of the basketball game. As different from a Hummer as . . . Tiffany from Amelia.

"No, of course not. I drove that one a couple of weeks just to humor Mother then traded it for a hybrid. Going green is best for the earth, you know."

"So Ricky asked you out when he stopped you?"

A hint of color flashed across her cheeks. "Actually, I asked him out. The Garden Society had a big do that weekend, and I had planned to go alone. He didn't know many folks in town, so he was glad to go with me. We hit it off so well, we've dated ever since. And I think he may be the one for me. I've dated some real losers, but I have a good feeling about Ricky. And it will really tick Mother off if I marry a police officer." She must have realized how that sounded, because she grimaced. "That's just the icing on the cake."

"Be careful, though. Dressing to aggravate

your mother is one thing, but marrying for that reason would be taking things a little too far."

A flash of irritation crossed her face.

Had I overstepped the bounds? After all, this was my boss I was giving advice to.

"That wouldn't be the reason. Like I said, it would just be a plus."

"I don't know. It seems like it would be a good idea to come to terms with your mother before you make permanent plans with anyone else."

"Is that Dear Pru speaking?" Sarcasm dripped from her voice.

"I've just seen too much unhappiness because of unresolved problems," I answered soberly. "Dear Pru sees a lot of sorrow. I've learned plenty from my readers."

"I'll think about it." She stood abruptly, and I followed her down the hall past the restrooms and break room. Tiffany pointed to a room near the door. "Do you realize that every newspaper Uncle Hank put out is in that room? If we were as up-to-date as most cities, it would all be on computer by now." She sighed. "But we're not."

I knew she was just trying to dispel the awkwardness my unwelcome advice had left between us, but I was curious. I pushed the door open and glanced inside at the rows of newspapers. "Wow. That's a lot of information."

"Yeah, probably forty years' worth at least. And all filed by date."

Wouldn't it be easy to solve a murder if I could organize my mind like this room?

While I was still daydreaming about that, Tiffany cleared her throat. "I've got to run."

As we exited the building, I thought about what I'd learned. Amelia's whole theory about her daughter not being able to attract men was skewed by her faulty perception of Tiffany. Sometimes I felt the same way about solving J.D.'s murder. Like there was a piece of the puzzle in plain sight that we just weren't seeing.

Dear Pru,

I am nearing thirty, and not to be cliché or anything, but my biological clock is ticking. I have met a man I really care for and am considering marrying him. He loves me, but I'm not sure if what I feel for him is love or if I am just settling so that I can have a family.

Not Sure

Not Sure,

If you aren't sure, there's a good chance you aren't in love. Only you can

140

decide if marrying a man you "like" in order to have a family is worth giving up on the real thing.

"Is this my favorite attorney?" I grinned as I imagined Alex on the other end of the phone line.

"It depends. Who's this?" he asked playfully.

"Your favorite waitress."

"Debbie?"

"Very funny."

"Oh wait! I recognize that sarcasm. This is Jenna, isn't it? Then, yes, this is your favorite attorney."

"Good, because I'm about to do something I've never done before and ask a man out on a date."

"Anyone I know?"

I snickered. "You're in rare form today, Counselor. Carly called, and she and Elliott want us to ride to Jonesboro with them to get some restaurant supplies." Before he could make a smart remark about how exciting that would be, I rushed on, "And eat at El Acapulco while we're there."

"That sounds good," Alex said.

An hour later, the four of us were on the road in Elliott's SUV and deep in discussion. With Elliott and Carly in the front seat and Alex and me in the middle seat, we covered everything from religion to politics, all those subjects you were supposed to avoid. How cool that we shared similar points of view on most things.

Halfway to Jonesboro, we started dissecting a Will Smith movie we had rented and watched together. Elliott glanced at Carly. "Keeping his identity a secret was what got him in trouble."

Carly jerked her head around to look at him. "He didn't do it on purpose at the beginning. And if she had known, she never would have gone out with him."

Elliott shrugged. "Still, keeping secrets like that keeps relationships from growing."

"Humph." Carly crossed her arms. "Shows how much you know. They ended up together, didn't they?"

Elliott kept his eyes on the road, but his knuckles were white on the steering wheel. Carly turned and looked out the passenger window.

Alex and I stared at each other in bewilderment. I shrugged. Elliott was just the brother-in-law I wanted. And I was pretty sure he was the husband Carly wanted. So what was the problem with these two lately? Sometimes they seemed thrilled to be together; other times they got upset with each other at the drop of a hat.

"So who do you think killed J. D. Finley?" I asked, more to break the silence than any real hope that my three traveling companions would know.

Nobody spoke for at least thirty seconds, then Elliott's death grip on the steering wheel slowly relaxed. "Well, I don't really know any of these folks very well. Lisa took a few lessons at the country club, and she struck me as a lady who knew what she wanted and how to get it." He kept his eyes on the road.

Carly glanced toward him. "That doesn't mean she'd kill someone, though. Lots of folks look out for number one. And they don't kill whoever gets in their way."

Oh boy. To think I'd been trying to smooth things over. "You're both right," I said. "And the suspect list is pretty sparsely populated. The only other person I've thought of so far is Larry."

"Who's Larry?" Elliott asked.

I told them about Larry and the way he had acted when he nearly ran me down at the gym. And how he'd yelled at Lisa.

"Sounds like a rough character," Elliott agreed. "And you think his motive would be jealousy? If he did it, I mean."

"I guess so. If we knew the motive, I think

we could figure out who did it." I glanced at Carly. "Unless it was a stranger like Carly hopes."

He nodded. "I agree with Carly. I don't like the thought of someone from Lake View being a cold-blooded killer."

I smiled at Alex. Finally, I'd found something they agreed on. He gave me a discreet thumbs-up.

At Sam's Club, Alex and I left Elliott and Carly to gather restaurant supplies while we wandered among the books and CDs. Before too long, Alex met a fellow lawyer, and they were soon engrossed in the intricacies of trout fishing: fly fishing versus live bait.

I listened for a while, but finally my attention span reached its limit.

"I'm going to go help Carly," I whispered and received an absent nod in response. "I'll call when we're done."

My stomach was growling, and I figured the sooner we got supplies taken care of, the sooner we could eat. A fajita was calling my name. I headed toward the back and had flipped my phone open to call Carly, when I heard her voice, strangely agitated. I closed the phone but could still hear her loud and clear. Apparently from the next aisle.

"I can't help it, Elliott. I don't think it's

the right thing to do."

"You think keeping secrets is the right thing? Come on, Carly. I think you're avoiding the issue. Your family is so close. How will they feel when you finally tell them? Someone, probably Jenna, will want to know when you found out. Then what?"

9

Barkin' up the wrong tree

I stayed out of sight but waited for my sister to answer. What was going on?

"I think I know my family better than you," Carly answered tartly.

"Fine." Elliott sounded more resigned than angry.

My curiosity meter was on full alert. Secrets? From the family? Did this have to do with the whole Travis situation? Or was there something else? And what was that "probably Jenna" crack about? I retraced my steps to Alex. I'd lost my desire to help gather supplies, as well as my appetite.

I was thankful Alex was alone when I found him. I quietly told him what I'd heard.

He put his arm around me, and I stood for a few seconds listening to his steady heartbeat. "I know it's hard," he said softly.

"But maybe this is something personal between the two of them. And that's really a good thing, isn't it? You *are* hoping that they're getting serious, right?"

"You mean like maybe they're about to get engaged and she isn't ready to tell us yet?"

He shrugged. "I don't know if that's it or not. But she'll tell you when she gets ready."

I nodded. "How do you do that?"

He raised an eyebrow. "What?"

"Make me feel better."

His dimple flashed. "It's a gift. Now let's find the secret-keeping couple and go eat."

I kissed him on the cheek. "Thanks."

"Anytime."

We met Elliott and Carly rolling two loaded carts toward the checkout. "Did you buy out the store?" Alex called, and they laughed. Any awkwardness I felt vanished. Alex was right. Carly would tell me when she was ready.

At the Mexican restaurant, my appetite returned with a vengeance. The swarthy young waiter brought chips and white cheese dip then took our order. He repeated each thing we said as he wrote it down and waited for a nod.

"He wants to be sure he gets it right, doesn't he?" I said after he left. As a newly minted waitress, I couldn't imagine how hard it must be to have a language barrier in addition to all of the other difficulties of the job.

"That reminds me of Vini," I said.

Carly nodded. "Speaking of Vini," she drawled, "I wonder if he has problems with his roommates or something. He acts like he never wants to go home."

"Yeah, I've noticed that, too. But he does a really good job," I said.

"I think because English isn't his native language, he pays close attention to all his orders. He makes fewer mistakes than . . ." She put her hand over her mouth and looked at me.

"What?" I looked right back. "I *know* you don't mean me."

"Of course I don't," Carly said. "I just realized it might be unprofessional to discuss my employees."

"So, who *do* you want to discuss?" Alex asked, and we all laughed.

I cleared my throat. "We could talk about employers."

"Now wait a minute," Carly drawled.

"I mean ex-employers, silly. I was just going to say that even though I'm sorry that it took Lisa getting in trouble to do it, I'm relieved that I've kind of made peace with Bob."

"Funny you should mention Bob and peace in the same sentence." Elliott dipped a chip in the cheese dip.

I frowned. "Why?"

He shrugged. "Just that I heard something weird out on the links this week." He stuck the chip in his mouth.

"About Bob?" Alex said.

Elliott nodded then chewed the chip for what seemed like forever. Maybe I was wrong about him being the perfect guy for Carly. Didn't he know I was dying of curiosity over here?

He swallowed. Finally. "I heard he and Wilma were full-fledged hippies back in the day. You know, peace, love, flower power. All that stuff."

"Like when they were teenagers?" Carly asked.

Elliott shook his head. "I honestly just heard bits and pieces, but I think it was more recent than that. Maybe when they were our age."

"So they were old hippies," Alex murmured.

"Speak for yourself," Carly and I said at the same time.

We grinned.

"Wonder what changed him?" I mused.

Elliott took a drink. "From what I heard, something big."

"What?" Carly pushed a jalapeño over to the side of her plate. "He got arrested for smoking pot?"

"I really don't know. More than one group of older men have alluded to it during golf games this week for some reason. But still, all I know is that apparently something bad happened out at Bob's place back then. And whatever it was, it put him on the straight and narrow." Elliott took the napkin off his lap and laid it beside his plate.

"I wonder why people are talking about that now," Carly said.

"Because Lisa's a suspect in a murder?" I suggested.

"Everything comes back to the murder with you, doesn't it, water girl?" Alex teased.

"I'm so glad you're feeling better, Mrs. Hanley." I hugged the tiny elderly woman gently. "We've missed you the last couple of weeks."

"It's good to be here." She beamed up at me. "When you're ninety-six, it's good to be anywhere." She laughed as much as I did over her joke. As I moved aside so others could welcome our congregation's oldest member back, I scanned the crowd for Alex.

Finally, I spotted him in the corner, in an earnest discussion with Mr. Foshee, the elder who taught Sunday morning Bible class. I sent up a silent but fervent prayer of thanks that the man I loved loved God.

"Jenna?" Mama appeared beside me. "You and Alex are coming to lunch, aren't you?"

My brows drew together, and I nodded. Didn't we always? Sunday afternoon at Stafford Cabins was a tradition since Carly and I'd moved back to town. I usually contributed green beans or corn, and Carly always brought some elaborate recipe she'd whipped up in her spare time.

"I've got a roast in the oven, but I don't have a salad. Since Carly's not going to be there, do you want to bring green beans *and* corn?"

"Sure I will. But what do you mean Carly's not going to be there?" Alex and I had playfully spent the ride to church guessing what culinary delight Carly might have cooked up for lunch today.

"Didn't she tell you?"

"I'm pretty sure she didn't." I'd been overworked and tired lately, but my mind hadn't quite gone on vacation yet.

Mama smiled. "I guess if she had, you'd have known. She and Elliott are eating together today. But the kids are coming to the house. Zac's taking them home to change out of church clothes and then bringing them on."

"She and Elliott? Alone? This sounds serious. Is it? What exactly did she tell you?" Maybe Carly had finally decided to act on the fact that Elliott was the man of her dreams.

"Jenna, please remember what curiosity did to the cat." Honestly, sometimes Mama treated me as if I were the twins' age. "Besides, she didn't say much. Just that she was eating with Elliott today because they had some things to discuss, and that Zac would bring the girls and come for lunch and basketball as usual. Now you know as much as I do."

"How did she look?"

Mama glanced around the auditorium then back at me with a frown. "What do you mean, 'How did she look?' She looked normal."

"Did she seem excited? Nervous? Happy? Or all of the above?"

"Jenna, you're a darling girl, and I love you very much, but you're slightly batty sometimes. Actually, she told me over the phone last night. But when she slipped into church a few minutes late this morning, she looked normal. That's the best I can do."

"I inherited my battiness from someone," I said with a cheeky grin. "Either I got it from you or you married a batty man. Take your choice." I patted her shoulder.

Without cracking a smile, she retorted, "You got it from your dad's great-uncle Jed. He was crazy as a Bessie bug."

I stared at her, and she started laughing. I joined her. The origin of my "battiness" might be in question. But there was no doubt where I got my sense of humor.

"Carly? It's Jenna. Call me when you get a chance." I hated leaving a message, but I was dying of curiosity. Me and the cat. I patted Neuro, who stretched and yawned before returning to licking her paw.

Okay. Just me.

The phone rang, and I snatched it up. "Hello?"

"Jenna? What's wrong?" Carly sounded groggy as if she'd just awakened. I glanced at the clock. Nope. It was ten o'clock on Sunday night. Not too late to call.

"Nothing's wrong. At least, nothing's wrong with me. Is something wrong with you?" I was babbling. "I mean, we missed you at lunch. Mama said you were with Elliott." Suggestive pause.

Silence on the other end of the line.

"Is he still there?"

"No."

"You want to talk?" Sometimes being blunt is the only way to find out what you want to know.

Silence. Then a hesitant, "If you do."

"I can be at your house in . . ." I decided I was decent in my sweats and a T-shirt, ". . . ten minutes." Who cared how I looked? My sister might have just gotten engaged. I had to know.

"Why?" Carly sounded bewildered.

"So you can tell me whatever it is you can't tell me on the phone."

"Jenna, what in the world is wrong with you? You're acting as crazy as —"

"Daddy's great-uncle Jed, I know. Mama's already told me."

"I must be dreaming." Carly had progressed — or regressed — from bewildered to completely befuddled. However, when she opened the door for me ten minutes later, she looked so normal that I had second thoughts about my engagement theory.

"Let's keep it low. The kids have school tomorrow, you know. They need their sleep. Besides . . ." She glanced around as if expecting a twin to pop up from behind the couch. "I don't want them to know about this right now."

That concerned face was not the face of a newly engaged woman. "Car, what's going on?"

She looked over her shoulder at the kids' rooms. "I can't really talk about it."

Suddenly, I remembered our conversation the day we played checkers on the porch. "Is this about Travis?" I mouthed.

She nodded and turned away. "But I don't know anything for sure. I should know everything in a few days, and I'll tell you then."

I knew she wouldn't lie to me, so no doubt she didn't know anything *for sure.* But the conversation I'd overheard on our trip to Jonesboro told me that she knew something she wasn't telling me. And unless I was mistaken, her eyes were red-rimmed. Short of whining and begging her to tell me, I had no choice but to give her a hug. "Fine. Tell me when you find out . . . for sure."

"I will," she said and guided me smoothly to the door. No doubt before I lost the tenuous hold I had on my curiosity.

"Pass the popcorn." I nudged Alex. We were watching one of my favorite movies, *Princess Bride.*

"As you wish." Alex handed me the nearly

empty bowl.

I elbowed him in the ribs. "Oh, that was cute." The movie had just come to the part where Grandpa explained that every time Westley said, "As you wish," to Buttercup, what he really meant was "I love you."

"I really do love you. You know that, don't you?" Alex turned toward me.

"If you really loved me, you would tell your boss that you're allergic to sunshine and beaches," I teased. He was leaving for a conference in Miami, and we were enjoying a last evening together before his departure the next morning.

Just as he leaned in for a kiss, the doorbell rang.

I grinned. "It's probably Zac. He said he'd try and come by and help me download some songs to my new phone."

"He can wait," Alex said softly and dropped a gentle kiss on my lips. Then he pushed to his feet. "I'll get the door, and you can refill the popcorn bowl."

"As you wish." I grinned over my shoulder at him as I headed to the kitchen. I stuck a bag in the microwave and turned it on. Over the popping I could hear a female voice interspersed with Alex's deeper male one. Not Zac, then.

Alex came into the kitchen, followed by

Gail. Her eyes were swollen, and her face was red and splotchy.

"Oh no. What's wrong?" I took the bag from the oven. "Was someone else murdered?"

She shook her head.

"I'll take Mr Persi out for a walk while you and Gail visit," Alex offered. Another thing I loved about Alex. He wasn't nosy like me.

"As you wish." I smiled at him. From the corner of my eye, I noticed Gail's puzzled expression. But it vanished immediately as tears came into her eyes.

"Oh, Jenna, I'm sorry to just drop by like this, but I didn't know what else to do." She pulled a paper towel from the holder on the counter and rubbed her face. "Lisa told the police that she was at work on Friday night during the time of the murder." She started crying. "But she wasn't. And she told me I'd get fired if I told the truth."

"Here, Gail." I motioned to a chair at the table. "Sit right here and let me get you some tea." I poured her tea and set the glass in front of her. "Where was she?" I shook the bag of popcorn into the bowl and offered it to her.

"I don't know. She left early without saying where she was going. She does it all the

time. Well, you know how she is, Jenna."
Gail absently took a piece of the popcorn.
"She never stays as long as she's supposed
to."

"Right. Nor does she do the work she
should do while she's there." I sat down
beside Gail. "So she threatened to fire you
if you said she wasn't there?"

She nodded. "I just don't know what to
do. I need that job, and besides, without
you there, the place would really fall apart
if I left, too." Tears rolled down her face.

"We have to tell Bob." I reached for my
cell phone. "Maybe he can get Lisa to tell
the truth. And I know he won't fire you." I
hit the arrow button down to the Bs. I raised
my eyebrows, and Gail nodded.

When Bob answered, I explained what
Lisa had done.

"I just can't believe she did that. Are you
sure?" Poor Bob. He just didn't want to face
the truth about his princess.

"I'm sure."

"This is going to look really bad for Lisa,
isn't it?" He was the master of understate-
ment. "What should we do?"

"Look, the only thing you can do is
convince Lisa to go see John. Have her tell
him she was scared and so she lied." I
glanced over at Gail to see if she agreed.

She nodded. "If Gail has to tell them, it will be even worse for Lisa. Also, she needs to tell them where she was."

Bob agreed, and we hung up. Gail stood and pushed her chair back to the table. "I feel so much better now. Thanks, Jenna."

I walked her to the door. "Don't worry, Gail. Bob and Lisa will go tomorrow to talk to John."

I heard the back door shut and knew Alex was back inside with Mr. Persi. Even though he didn't ask, I told him what Gail had said and Bob's response.

When I finished, I frowned. "I wonder where she really was, though."

"Of course you do, honey. I'm sure the police will find out." Alex guided me back toward the living room. "Let's finish the movie."

After Alex left, I called and told Carly about Lisa's false alibi. "Where do you think Lisa was?" she wondered aloud.

"I think we need to find out. Don't you?"

"I'd like to tell you that you need to mind your own business, but I don't think that'll happen. And, after all, the murder did happen on my property. Let's just try and stay safe this time, okay?"

"Of course." It's not like I wanted to be face-to-face with a murderer. Again.

10

If it ain't your tail, don't wag it.

Just like every day since the murder, I parked in the back of the diner parking lot as far away from the Dumpster as I could. I always had the creepy feeling that if I looked behind the Dumpster, I would see that little sports car. With a dead man in the front seat. I hurried inside, trying not to glance in that direction.

But just like every day, the questions ran through my head. Who killed J. D. Finley and why? Why behind a Dumpster? I could think of plenty of answers for the first question, but I couldn't imagine why J.D. was parked behind the Dumpster at the diner.

As soon as I opened the door, the delicious scent of apples and cinnamon made my mouth water. Alice was expertly cutting the edges off the top crust of an apple pie. She opened the oven door and put the scallop-edged pie in with several others already turning golden brown.

As I headed into the dining room, I snagged an apron off the hook and tied it around my waist. I grabbed an order pad off the shelf, stuck a couple of pens in my pocket, then looked around at the many empty tables scattered throughout the diner. I waved at John, sitting in a booth alone and in uniform. "We don't seem quite as full today as we have been."

"It's Tuesday." Debbie offered no other explanation.

"And that means . . ." That people aren't hungry? Everyone runs home for lunch? What?

She left me waiting while she took a piece of fresh apple pie over to John. When she came back, she said, "Oh, I figured you knew. A couple of the fast-food places have big Tuesday specials. This is usually our slowest day."

Seeing John gave me an idea. I could get Amelia off my back and use some easy questions about Ricky to get a conversation going with John. Then I would segue neatly into how the murder investigation was going. "Hey, I'm going to take a quick break."

Her brows drew together, and I could see she was thinking about the fact that I'd just arrived, but she shrugged. "Whatev."

I slid into the booth across from the police chief. "We need to talk."

He froze with a bite halfway to his mouth. "Look, Jenna, if this is about the murder, legally I can't tell you anything. When are you going to understand that?"

"This is your lucky day, then. Because my question has nothing to do with the murder."

He looked skeptical but put the bite in his mouth. "What?" he said as he chewed.

"It's about Ricky . . ."

"Ricky? My officer Ricky?"

I nodded. "Okay, I might as well just explain it. Amelia asked me to ask around about Ricky and see what people know about him."

John's face grew alarmingly red, and for a minute I was afraid I was going to have to do the Heimlich maneuver.

"Because of Tiffany, you know," I said hurriedly. "I wouldn't have agreed, but I owe her a favor."

He snorted. "The first lady isn't ever going to think anyone is good enough for her daughter."

"I know that." I was a little ashamed that I'd even agreed to ask, but I had. So I needed to find out something. "Maybe you could tell me something that would reassure her."

"I think Ricky's a good officer and a stand-up guy. He knows what he's doing and doesn't mind doing it. We were short-handed when he applied. Frankly, he was an answer to a prayer."

I nodded. "Anything else?"

He leaned forward. "Yes."

"What?" I leaned forward, too.

"I thought this pie was free. I didn't know I was going to have to answer a question for every bite."

I tossed my hair over my shoulder and gave him a mock glare. "Fine. Enjoy your pie." I slid to my feet. John couldn't even answer my questions without getting smart when they had nothing to do with the murder. No way was I going to get any pertinent information from him about J.D. Might as well not even ask.

I walked back into the kitchen to cool off. Carly turned from where she was dishing up chicken and dumplings. "What's wrong?"

"John. He won't cut me any slack."

She turned back to the stove. "In other words, he won't give you any information."

"Basically. Anyway, I'm officially going to work now. While I was talking to John, I noticed people are starting to come in."

She grinned. "Slowly but surely we're overcoming the slow Tuesday curse."

When I walked back into the dining room, more than half the tables were full. The word about Carly's cooking was spreading. I quickly got into the rhythm of taking orders and delivering plates heaped with today's specials.

I mentally congratulated myself on doing such a good job. So far I hadn't dropped anything or switched any orders. Although I did fumble a plate when I glanced over toward Vini's section where Harvey had seated Bob and Wilma. I wasn't sure what the etiquette was when seeing your ex-boss after you'd just found out he'd had an unusual past. Knowing he'd been a hippie in another life, I could easily envision him with a long braid and headband, à la Willie Nelson. I resisted the urge to flash him and Wilma a peace sign.

Just as I made up my mind to go over and say hello, Bob jumped up and shook his finger in Vini's face. I couldn't hear the words, but even from a distance it was obvious this wasn't a friendly conversation.

I hurried over just as Vini backed up a couple of steps, his dark eyes wide in his ashen face. "I did not kill him. Why would you say that?" By now people at other tables were craning their necks to see what was going on. I stepped between them.

"Hi, Bob." I nodded toward Wilma. "And Wilma." She gave me a weak smile and waggled her fingers toward me. "Something wrong?" I turned toward Vini. "Why don't you go on and put their order in?" I pointed toward his order pad. "Maybe you can discuss this after they finish eating and there aren't quite so many people here."

Bob looked around the crowded room, his face reddening. He sat down quickly. Vini headed toward the kitchen.

"Is Lisa doing any better?"

"At least she isn't in jail." Wilma answered for Bob, who had his head down. "But now the police just won't leave her alone." She looked over toward the table where Seth and Ricky were enjoying their free pie after their lunch. "They act like they think *she* killed J.D."

"But she didn't!" Bob jerked his head up and slapped his hand on the table. "Vini was the one who had a big fight with him. If he lets my little girl take the rap for something he did, I'll . . . I'll . . ."

"Bob. Stop." Wilma put her hand over his. "Jenna knows Lisa didn't kill him. And if Vini did, well, John or those other policemen will find out."

"So why would you think Vini did it?" I couldn't imagine the soft-spoken foreign student killing anyone. Or even getting angry with anyone.

"You know they worked together at the club. J.D. caught him stealing from the cash register, and Lisa fired him."

"Lisa fired Vini for stealing?" Why wouldn't Gail have told me that?

"Yes." Bob worried the napkin wrapped around his silverware. "So maybe Vini hated him." He glanced up at me. "And maybe he hates Lisa, too." He sounded shocked at the thought that anyone could hate his darling daughter.

"Now, Bob." Wilma patted Bob's hand. "Everyone loves Lisa." I guess Mama was right when she said there's no love like a mother's love.

He flashed his wife a look that said a father's love was just as strong, but maybe not quite so blind. "Anyway, just because it was her gun, they think she did it." He shook his head. "She told the police someone stole her gun a few days before the murder, but they act like they don't believe her." He took out each piece of his silverware and laid it on the table as if his hands couldn't keep still.

"Well, she doesn't know exactly when it was stolen, does she?" I asked.

He frowned. "She kept it at work in the desk drawer. It's not like she pulled it out all the time." His eyes brightened. "Maybe Vini stole it when he took the money."

"Do you know anyone who didn't like J.D? Anyone besides Vini who had had an argument with him?" I just couldn't believe Vini would kill anyone, but if I had learned anything, it was that you can't tell a murderer by the way he looks. Or acts.

"Well." Bob and Wilma exchanged a look. "Harvey . . ." He froze.

"Harvey? Harvey what?"

Wilma cleared her throat and looked over my shoulder.

I glanced back. Harvey was walking up behind me. "Hey, Harvey, what's up?" I slid my pad and pen into my pocket and turned to face him.

"Jenna, aren't you supposed to be working? This isn't even one of your tables. People are starting to complain." His glare included me and Bob. "We've always prided ourselves on good service. I'd hate to think that now that we've sold, that's all a thing of the past."

"Oh my goodness." I'd let my curiosity get me in trouble. Again. And after I had just been bragging to myself about how good I was doing. "Excuse me, y'all. I'll go get your food and then get back to my tables."

As I walked away, Harvey muttered, "Hippie troublemaker." I glanced back at him, but he was stomping away. I remembered what I'd told Elliott on our trip to Jonesboro. It really was odd that suddenly everyone was talking about Bob's flower-child past.

I found Vini, who looked relieved when I suggested that he trade Bob and Wilma's table for one of mine.

Later, when I laid the ticket on Bob's table and turned to go, Bob touched my arm. "Jenna, I know you're helping your sister out here, but do you think there is any way you could work some at the club?" His humble tone touched my heart. "Lisa's so upset that she can't really do much work."

What was her excuse before? I bit my tongue to keep the words from coming out. Mama always told me you shouldn't kick a man when he's down. And Bob was so down, he was practically subterranean.

"To be honest," Wilma said softly, "Lisa's so sad and upset that she's taken to her bed."

Well, then. If Lisa wasn't going to be at

the club pretending to work, I'd be glad to help out. "Carly just hired a new waitress, so I was planning to cut back on my hours here anyway, Bob." I stuck my pad in my apron pocket. "I can work if you need me. I'll stop by tomorrow and pick up a key."

Carly was just grabbing her keys to head out the door when I finished the noon shift. As we walked out together, I told her about Bob asking me to work.

"Would you mind if I cut my hours back so I can help Bob out?" I glanced over at her. "Be honest."

"No, of course not. I don't blame you at all." She stopped beside her car. "But are you sure you're not letting your sympathy put you back in a bad position?"

I shrugged. "I'm not sure, but I just feel so sorry for them." I stopped. "You know I've really enjoyed working at the diner. More than I ever thought I would." I opted for total honesty. "But I guess I didn't realize how much I'd miss the club."

"I understand. Of course you miss it."

"By the way . . ." I glanced around to make sure no one could overhear me. "I found something else out today that I need to tell you."

"What?" She looked around the crowded parking lot.

I lowered my voice. "Remember the other day when Vini was talking about how broke he was and how much it cost for his school?"

She nodded.

"Well, today Bob said that Lisa fired Vini for stealing from the cash register at the club."

Carly gasped. "I can't believe that." She shook her head. "He seems so trustworthy. Are you sure this isn't another of Lisa's 'stories'?"

"I'll ask Gail if she knows what happened. If anyone would know, she would."

"Let me know what she says."

Dave, the personal trainer and weight room manager, was working the desk when I walked into the health club. When he said Gail didn't come in until three, I headed back to the pool room. After some relaxing laps, I was about to head for the sauna, when the steamed-up glass doors opened and Gail walked in.

"Hey, girl, Dave said you're looking for me."

"Guilty as charged." I grabbed a couple of towels and wrapped one around my hair and another around my body. "Do you have a minute to talk?"

170

She nodded. "Sure. My shift doesn't start for another ten minutes. What's on your mind?"

I sat down in a white deck chair and waved her to the one beside it. Déjà vu. Just call me Amelia. I hoped I hadn't motioned Gail as imperiously as Amelia had me a few days ago.

When we were seated, I smiled at her. "I need to talk to you about Vini."

Her eyes widened. "Why? What about him?" she asked. She looked so alarmed that I faltered. Had I been wrong about Vini?

"Bob mentioned that he was fired from the club for stealing. Is that right?"

She relaxed in her chair and snorted. "That's the excuse Lisa gave. But it isn't true."

"Can you tell me what happened?"

"Not to speak ill of the dead or anything, but J.D. was a jerk. And Lisa just followed him around like a puppy dog. I know it made Bob sick to watch them."

"What do you mean? I thought Bob liked him."

"Ha. No way. Bob couldn't stand him. Actually, that's what started the whole thing with Vini. I heard Bob tell Lisa that since membership enrollment was down, we'd have to let someone go." She raised an eyebrow at me. "When you left, so did members."

I felt my cheeks grow hot at the implied praise. No doubt the mass exodus of members was more because of Lisa's inept management than because of the absence of my amazing management skills. "Go ahead."

"Anyway, he told her to get rid of one employee. No matter what Bob intended, he should have known she wouldn't fire her man. So she and J.D. cooked up this little story to get Vini fired."

"How do you know it isn't true?"

"I counted the cash in the register that night. Then I checked with the bank to see how much the deposit was. Every penny was deposited."

"Wow. So do you think they wanted to get rid of Vini specifically? Or just any employee so J.D. could stay on?"

"I think they picked on Vini because they knew he wouldn't fight them on it. Plus, he hadn't been here as long as the rest of us. I'm so glad you hired him at the diner."

"Me, too. So you weren't a fan of J.D.'s?"

"Nope. He and Bob had some kind of history, too. Did you know that?"

"No. What kind of history?"

"I'm not sure. I just heard him say something about telling Lisa about 'our shared past.' I was under the impression that he may have been holding something over Bob's head." She shrugged. "You know, threatening Bob. But I can't imagine why."

"Me either." But I was certainly going to find out.

When she left, I retired to the sauna. In the steamy quietness, I sat for a minute and mulled over the life and death of J.D. Finley. When he drove to the Dumpster, did he have death on his mind? Did he have an appointment with a murderer? Or had it been a surprise attack?

I rolled up a towel for a pillow and stretched out on my back on the hot wooden bench. Closing my eyes, I worked my way down my mental suspect list. Even though Lisa owned the murder weapon, why would she have done it? Had J.D. proven hard to shake as a boyfriend? That seemed a flimsy excuse for murder. More in keeping with Lisa's personality would be if J.D. were the one trying to get out of the relationship. I could see her, in a fit of anger, using her toy gun to take care of the problem. But I couldn't see her keeping it to herself and playing the innocent so well. She really didn't act guilty at all. What if someone really had stolen her gun? The more I thought about it, the more likely that seemed.

And who better than her husband, who seemed like a raving maniac when I'd seen him at the club the other day. And he definitely knew where the gun was. Any man who would beat his wife might also kill her lover. How closely were the police looking at Larry?

My eyes fluttered as I suddenly remembered what Gail had just told me about Bob. It sounded like my ex-boss had motives of his own for getting rid of J.D. The only thing that didn't add up there was him letting his precious princess take the fall.

I sat up and punched my rolled-up towel a couple of times to fluff it again and stretched back out. I wasn't having much luck with the relaxing part of this little sauna visit.

So many people were acting weird. Debbie, even Carly — not that I thought hers had anything to do with the murder — and of course, Vini. He seemed flustered so much of the time, and often he acted like he didn't want to leave the diner. I'm not sure what was wrong about that, but it just felt odd.

On the other hand, he'd hardly had the opportunity to commit murder unless he'd excused himself to go to the bathroom and slipped out back, shot J.D., then slipped in to work without anyone noticing. Which was possible, yes. But probable, no.

And what about motive? He obviously resented J.D. getting him fired, but was the soft-spoken, mild-mannered student capable of cold-blooded murder? And framing Lisa for his actions? I didn't think so. And since I'd had a hard time believing he would steal, and from what Gail said, I was right, I tended to go with my gut feeling about Vini.

11

Lettin' the cat out of the bag is a lot
easier'n puttin' it back in.

Closing time. Finally. Carly had sent Debbie and Susan home already, and Vini and I were gathering the last of the garbage. Since the night Vini told Carly how badly he needed hours — and proven how well he could clean the men's bathroom — he'd helped clean up.

"You know my new rule. I do not, under any circumstances, take out the garbage." I twisted the tie and set the full bag by the door. "Just let me close this other bag, and you can carry them both out."

As I pulled the black bag out of the metal can, I noticed a flash of light. It almost looked like a flashlight had come on inside the bag. I donned some heavy cleaning gloves from under the sink and stuck my hand in to fish it out. When I reached for it,

I saw it was my cell phone. It must have fallen out of my apron pocket when I was cleaning and landed in one of the garbage cans. I was thankful that when the side buttons get bumped, it lights up. Otherwise I'd have lost it forever. I wiped it off with a paper towel.

"What do you think? Some of these are pretty sturdy." I showed it to Carly. "Even though it looks like it's on, I don't want to mess with it while it's so nasty. Do you think it will still work after I take it apart and clean it off? I was just learning how to use it."

"Not to mention all that music Zac said he put on it for you." Carly hung her dish towel on the towel rack. "It might be worth cleaning it and trying it out."

Vini picked up the bags and headed out the back door while I took the back off the phone and cleaned the outside of it with a damp paper towel. The inside still looked good as new. I put the battery back in, hit the power button, and was rewarded with the little orange man doing cartwheels across the screen. "Yea! It still works."

I hit the envelope for text messages to see if Alex had messaged me while I was at work. The first received message said, "Waiting for you out back."

"How in the world could he be waiting for me out back?" I held up the phone where Carly could read the message. "His plane left this morning."

"No idea." She shrugged. It hit us both at the same time. The last time someone was waiting out back . . . Was a murderer waiting for me out back? But why would he warn me?

We both jumped up. "Vini!" we screamed in unison. I ran toward the back door with Carly on my heels. We screeched to a halt at the door and looked at each other. Would we find his body on the ground behind the diner?

I pulled the door open and peeked out. "Vini? Are you okay?" No answer. Carly gave me a little shove.

I held on to her sleeve and dragged her out on the back porch with me. "Vini!" I yelled louder. "Where are you?"

Vini strolled up from the side of the diner. "What is wrong, Jenna? You sound upset."

"Where were you? I was worried that something may have happened to you." My voice trembled.

"I went to get my phone out of my van. I forgot it there." He held up a cell phone. "I was going to call Gail."

"Oh." While the two of them were with

178

me, I felt brave enough to look all around the back alley that adjoined the diner parking lot — from the safety of the back porch, of course. As far as I could see, there wasn't a car or another human in sight.

Vini walked into the diner ahead of us. I tugged on Carly's sleeve. "I don't think this is my phone."

"Why?"

I told her quickly about the phone mix-up with Debbie when we were remodeling. As soon as we got back into the light, I checked the outbox. There were several sent messages. None looked familiar. I occasionally sent texts, but I hadn't sent these. The most recent ones said, "Did you leave?" and "Why won't you answer?" There were several that sounded about the same. I hit the button to bring up the address book. Only one number. Very strange. It was listed as "Me." The same thing the screen had said when I'd used her phone the last time I'd gotten it by mistake — "Connected to Me."

I waited until we finished up and Vini was in the break room gathering his things, then I showed the phone to Carly. "You think I should take it to her tonight?"

"No. She'll be here tomorrow." She carefully locked the front door. "Aren't you working the noon shift?"

I nodded.

"Well, just give it to her then."

"See you both tomorrow," Vini called as he left.

Out in the parking lot, I stopped. "Car? Who do you think was waiting?"

"What?" She hit the remote and opened her van door. "See you tomorrow."

"Wait." I put out a hand to restrain her. "Who was waiting for Debbie in the back?"

"The only person in the back was —" A look of comprehension flooded her face. "You think J.D. was waiting for Debbie? But why? I mean, he and Lisa were dating."

"That would explain why he was behind the Dumpster. He was cheating on Lisa with Debbie."

Carly frowned. "That's so cliché. Your boyfriend cheating with your best friend."

"Yeah. I hate to think that Debbie was doing that."

She shrugged. "It happens a lot, though. Now that I think about it, things are cliché because they're common. And as far as I know, J.D. and Lisa were just dating, not engaged."

"Yeah, but Lisa doesn't strike me as one who would take it so well if the man she was dating wanted to date someone else. I wonder if she knew. If she did, would she be mad enough to —" I couldn't finish the thought. Murder is such an ugly word.

"Didn't Lisa meet J.D. when she went with Debbie to his grandmother's funeral? Maybe Debbie felt like he belonged to her and Lisa just horned in. You know, maybe she felt justified. Or maybe there was nothing going on. He could've had a perfectly innocent reason to text that to Debbie."

"Yeah? Name one."

"Well . . ." She thought a minute then rose to the challenge. "Maybe he and Debbie were planning a surprise party for Lisa. Or maybe he wanted Debbie's advice about a gift he was buying for Lisa. Or maybe he was going to ask Debbie about Lisa's husband, or . . ."

"Okay, I get it." I slapped her arm lightly. "I think we should take this to Debbie tonight and find out what it's all about."

"Jen, I'm worn out. I have three kids waiting at home. She can get it tomorrow. The messages will still be there. We can ask her then."

"We'll be so busy we won't have time. Besides, I want to know tonight."

"That's you to the bone. I've gotta know, and I've gotta know now." She grinned at me, but it was a tired grin. "I'm sorry. I just can't go tonight." She yawned widely, covering her mouth with her hand. "I'm nearly dead on my feet."

"No prob. You run on home and get some rest. You look beat."

As she drove off, I considered my options — wait until tomorrow or run by Debbie's tonight. Easy choice.

As I pulled into Debbie's driveway, a light in the living room went off. I parked and walked onto the front porch, clutching the phone. The motion light beside the front door came on, and I jumped then snickered at my nervousness.

I pushed the doorbell button. No response. Since I hadn't actually heard a chime, I decided the bell might be broken. I knocked. And waited. If I hadn't seen the light go off as I drove up, I would have thought nobody was home. Instead, I felt sure that Debbie just didn't want to see anyone. I squinted at the bright porch light shining in my face and glanced down at the phone in my hand.

Didn't want to see anyone?

Or me, in particular?

The conversation at every table was the same. Just one time today I would like to take an order or deliver food to someone who was talking about something besides whether or not the police were going to arrest Lisa. Anything else would do. I'd even settle for hearing about a NASCAR race. Anything but the possibility of poor Lisa going to jail. But that didn't keep me from listening and trying to sift the truth from gossip.

When Harvey sat Marge and Tiffany at a table in my section, I hurried over to take their order. On the way back to the kitchen, a teen was entertaining his buddies. "I heard she was a serial killer and killed at least five people."

At another table I heard an older woman talking about "all those drugs they were using." As far as I knew, Lisa was not a drug user. But what about J.D.? And I didn't catch everything the woman with her said, but it was something about "the sins of the fathers." I wondered whose father she was referring to but couldn't figure out a way to ask her without appearing nosy. Okay, nosier than usual.

A few minutes later, I set Marge's salad down on the table. As I handed Tiffany her salad, I thought about the fact that she had ordered a salad when she was with Marge instead of the "fat-filled" burger she had ordered when she was with her mother.

"I'm really worried about Lisa. Do you know if they're going to arrest her?"

Marge glanced up at me. "I've heard several rumors, Jenna. Hopefully we'll get a police report in time to put the truth in the paper." She glanced at Tiffany. "But one of our sources said they found a towel with the victim's blood on it in her car."

A bloody towel in Lisa's car? How had I not found out about this? I tried to cover my dismay. "Did either of you know him? J.D?" I set their salad dressings on the table. "I heard he was from here originally."

"I knew his grandmother pretty well. And of course I remember all the scandal during his trial."

"Trial?" My voice rose, and a few people glanced toward us. Oh well, anyone who overheard probably just thought I was talking about Lisa's future like everyone else. "Why did he have a trial?"

"I guess you were too young to remember." She paused and tapped her chin thoughtfully. "Well, maybe you weren't even born yet. I've lost track of the years, but it happened a long time ago." She settled her napkin in her lap. "I don't think he served any time." Again she paused. "Hmm. Maybe just probation since he was a minor." If this were anyone but Marge, I would think she was drawing this out on purpose to frustrate me.

"So what'd he do?" Mama was right. Too much curiosity could drive you crazy.

She glanced around the diner. "This isn't the best place to discuss it." She lowered her voice. "You can ask your mother or dad later. I'm sure they remember."

They probably did remember, but Mama had distinctly asked me not to get involved in this investigation. So asking them was out of the question.

Just as I opened my mouth to reply, I heard a loud crash behind me. I spun around. Debbie stood with her hand to her mouth. Broken plates and the remains of more than one daily special littered the floor. Except for the part that was spread down the front of Grimmett and one of his friends.

"Excuse me, ladies. I think I'm needed over there." I snatched a stack of napkins on my way over to the mess. Debbie's lips were trembling, and tears welled in her eyes as she tried to wipe chicken and dressing off Grimmett's shirt. He pushed her hands away and took a napkin from me and handed one to his friend. Debbie stepped back.

Alice hurried out of the kitchen with two

damp towels. She handed one to Debbie, who took it and started wiping at the food. Alice bent down beside her and helped. Vini rushed over with a tray, and he and I picked up the broken plates.

Grimmett and his equally unlucky friend got most of the food off their shirts. He turned back to his buddies as if we weren't there. "So like I was saying . . . I heard she caught him in that little sports car with another woman and shot him."

Vini and I exchanged a skeptical look as we finished up cleaning. Right. Parked behind the Dumpster with his secret love. How romantic. And even if he were, where was this mysterious other woman when I found the body?

Grimmett must have had the same thought. He glanced down at me. "Is that true? Since you found the body, you oughta know."

I rose to my feet and dusted my hands off over the tray. "I didn't see anyone else."

"I'm going to try and clean some of this off my apron." Debbie's tears had dried some, but she was still ashen. "Can you cover my tables for a few minutes?"

I looked around the crowded dining room. "I'll try. You go ahead."

I was really busy, but once again Vini and

I were able to cover Debbie's tables as well as our own. By the time I realized she wasn't coming back, our shift was over. Now I'd have to run her phone by her house again.

I walked into the break room to gather my things and smiled when I saw Harvey and Alice there drinking a cup of coffee. Suddenly, I had a brilliant idea. I poured myself a cup and sank down beside them.

"How's everything going?" I asked conversationally.

Harvey nodded. "Pretty good."

"Still planning to move to Florida after you finish helping Carly?"

Alice tilted her head as if she could see through my casual questions. "Planning on it."

"I need to ask y'all a question."

"Ookay," Harvey said.

I smiled. "Marge told me to ask my parents for the details, but frankly, Mama's already lectured me about staying out of this murder investigation, so I thought I'd ask you two instead. It's about J.D."

Alice jerked, and her hot coffee splashed down her hand and onto the table.

"Oh no." She clutched her hand.

"Are you okay?" I asked quickly.

Harvey jumped up and grabbed her. "Here, hon, let's get some cold water on that." He bustled her out of her chair to the staff bathroom while I wiped up the mess.

I went to get a damp rag from the kitchen, and when I came back, the couple was nowhere in sight. Had Harvey taken Alice to the ER for her burn? Or were they hiding out to avoid any further questioning? Maybe the whole town was in on some sort of cover-up about J.D.'s past. Or maybe I'd been watching too many old movies.

After Alice's strange reaction, if it was a reaction, taking Debbie's phone back shifted to second on my priority list. First, I had to find out what Marge had been talking about. With that in mind, I looked up her number in my address book. After all, Marge hadn't said she wouldn't tell me; she'd just said the diner wasn't the place to discuss it. Maybe her house would be. One phone call later, I'd been invited by for a glass of tea.

Ten minutes later, still smelling like the lunch specials, I walked up to Marge's door. Had it only been a year ago that I'd stood on this same porch holding a green bean casserole after Hank's murder? So much had changed. Some for the better, some for the worse. I reached out to ring the doorbell, and the sun glinted off my engagement ring.

One change in particular was a definite improvement.

Marge opened the door and motioned for me to come in. I stepped past her into a house that only remotely resembled the one she and Hank had lived in. Just as she'd done with her personality since she'd become a widow, Marge had opened up the house to sunshine and light. Bright cheery colors replaced the drab beige walls, and as she ushered me into the living room, the plastic-covered couch was nowhere to be found. "I love what you've done with the place," I murmured as I sank onto an over-stuffed red chair.

Her face lit up. "Really? Tiffany helped me. She and I had so much fun picking everything out. We even did most of the work ourselves. But the ideas and the planning were all hers. She's a genius with colors."

I shook my head as I thought of Tiffany's drab wardrobe, dull, frizzy hair, and scrubbed face. Behind that costume, she hid a flair for colors and design. That girl had learned a long time ago how to choose her weapons in the perpetual battle with her mother. "It's wonderful, Marge."

She beamed and sank down onto the loveseat. "So what are you curious about this time?" She took a sip of her tea.

"You mentioned J.D.'s 'trial.' And I couldn't ask Mama and Daddy." I told her quickly about Mama's warning to me to stay out of the murder investigation.

She nodded and went to set her tea glass down.

"So I asked Harvey and Alice."

Marge jostled her glass and almost dropped it. Tea splashed onto the coffee table. She jumped up and snatched a tissue from a dispenser on the end table. "Oh, good heavens, Jenna! Why would you ask Harvey and Alice? They were the very reason I didn't tell you in the diner." She wiped up the liquid and gave me a measured look. "How'd they react?"

I nodded toward her tea. "Alice reacted just like you did, actually. Only hers was hot coffee."

"Ouch," Marge mouthed. "Is she okay?"

"I think so. When I came back from getting a cloth to wipe up the spill, they were gone."

"Of course they were."

"Why? What is J.D. to them?"

She leaned her head back against the chair and stared at the tri-fold screen as if seeing the past unfolding on it. "Harvey and Alice's only daughter was killed in a car accident."

"When?" I'd known they had one child who died young, but I'd never heard details.

Lost in thought, Marge counted on her fingers then brought her gaze back to me. "Next month, it'll be thirty years."

"What does that have to do with J.D.?"

"He was the one responsible for her death."

And obviously he had a trial. "So he did time?"

Marge shrugged. "I don't remember, exactly. I think they put him in some kind of lockup, but he was a minor, so it was probably a place for juvenile delinquents. Believe it or not, we never talked about him again after his trial."

"Never?"

She shrugged. "Hank put a few articles about his case in the paper, even though I begged him not to. Now I can see that he had no choice, but I was younger then and more naive."

"But the rest of the town just acted as if he didn't exist?"

"Everyone thought that the best thing for Harvey and Alice was to just put it behind them and pretend the accident never happened. Even J.D.'s own grandmother — God rest her soul — felt guilty the rest of her life." She stood and grabbed another tissue. "Back then not talking about it was how people dealt with grief." She wiped her eyes. "It was probably the wrong thing, but it was all we knew to do."

"What happened exactly?"

She considered my question then pushed to her feet. "Honey, I'm just not willing to dredge up the past. We're talking about wounds that are as old as you are. And any healing that has been done is tenuous, at best. Far be it from me to stir things up again."

I could tell I was being dismissed, so I reluctantly stood. Sure enough, she walked toward the front door, and I followed. "But now with J.D. murdered . . ."

She held open the front door and shook her head. "I refuse to think that anybody killed that boy because of what happened thirty years ago."

Out on the porch, I considered her parting statement. "I wish I could be so sure," I murmured to myself as I walked slowly to my car. "I just wish I could be so sure."

12

Your chickens will come home to roost.

"So basically, what you're saying is that you want me to drive the getaway car?" Carly asked.

I plopped down in the chair with my mail on my lap and started slitting envelopes. "That makes it sound like I'm doing something wrong. All I want to do is give Debbie's phone back to her."

"And find out why she was meeting J.D. the night he died and why she didn't come forward with that information." Carly's flippant tone came through my little phone loud and clear.

Before I could answer, she continued, "Oh, and ask her why exactly she put the phone at the bottom of the trash."

"Basically," I said in a small voice, looking at an invitation to Tiffany's wedding shower at the country club.

"Sure," Carly said, apparently resigned to life with my avid curiosity. "I'll pick you up in ten minutes."

"Thanks."

When she pulled up in front of my house fifteen minutes later, I was on the porch waiting. I ran out and jumped in the passenger seat. "You're late."

"Beggars can't be choosers."

"Hey!" I protested with a grin. "Just because I'm trying to do the smart thing and take someone with me when I go to confront a person who may or may not be a homicidal maniac . . ."

The word *homicide* reminded me of the disturbing news I'd learned from Marge earlier, and my grin faded. I quickly filled Carly in.

She wiped at tears with one hand and drove with the other. "How awful for Harvey and Alice."

"I know," I said quietly, handing her a tissue. "And I wonder how taking a life, whether accidentally or on purpose, affected J.D. It must have changed the course of his life."

"Yeah," Carly agreed. "Especially if even his grandmother didn't mention his name anymore."

"Ironic that he came back for her funeral

and ended up getting killed, isn't it?" I wondered again if trouble had followed him to our sleepy little town of Lake View. Or if it had been here waiting for him all along.

I knocked on the door of Debbie's tiny house and cast a glance over my shoulder to where Carly waited in her car with the engine running.

When Debbie opened the door a crack, I shoved the cell phone toward her. "I accidentally got your phone again."

She recoiled and shook her head, still not opening the door all the way. "That's not my phone."

"It's the phone you had at the diner the other day." I held it up again to show her. "Remember when we got our phones mixed up?"

"That doesn't belong to me." She opened the door a little more. "I'm telling you, it isn't mine." Her voice rose.

"I know why you don't want to claim it. You might as well come out here so we can talk about it." I really didn't want her to invite me in. I was so jumpy these days, I was seeing a killer on every familiar face.

She hesitated, and for a minute I thought she might slam the door shut and dead bolt herself inside. But slowly she opened the door and stepped outside.

Her hair was matted on one side and her face creased. I could tell she'd been sleeping, or more likely from the looks of her red eyes, lying in bed crying.

Whatever the truth of the situation was, my heart ached for her. "You need to take this phone to John and explain where you got it."

"No, Jenna. I can't do that." Debbie sounded near hysterics. "You just don't understand."

"I think I do. You and J.D. were seeing each other behind Lisa's back, right?" I checked again to make sure Carly was still there.

"Not really."

"He gave you a cell phone to call him on, but you weren't seeing each other?" I'd figured that much out on the way over, when I'd realized that the one number in the phone that was put in as "Me" had to be J.D.'s. He must have added it in himself and given Debbie the phone. The police had questioned Lisa about whether she had another phone. No doubt they'd found the text messages on J.D.'s phone, but since this phone was also in J.D.'s name, the police didn't know who had it.

"We . . ." She choked out the words. "We

kept telling ourselves we were just friends and that Lisa just wouldn't understand us hanging out. But the truth was I was falling in love with him. And I think he was with me, too."

"So why didn't you just tell her?"

"Neither of us wanted to hurt Lisa." She blinked rapidly against the tears filling her eyes, but they spilled down her cheeks anyway.

My guess was that J.D. didn't want to lose his job at the health club, but I could have been wrong.

"We were going to tell her Sunday, but he got killed before we got the chance." She swiped at her eyes with the back of her hand.

"So you threw the phone away?"

"Yes," Debbie spat out the word. Then her voice broke. "And it tore my heart out to do it." She cried harder. "It was my last link with J.D." She was sobbing so hard now, I could barely understand her. "If Lisa killed him, it's my fault." She dug a tissue out of her pocket and wiped her nose.

"Debbie, how could it be your fault?"

"Maybe Lisa found out about us and got mad and killed him." Debbie sobbed.

"If she did, John needs this phone. You should take it to him and tell him about you and J.D."

"No," she said flatly. "I won't. If Lisa doesn't already know and she found out, it would ruin our friendship. And I'm the only friend she has left now."

"I'll have to take it to John. How long do you think it will take for them to find out it was yours?"

"That's just it. It wasn't mine. Like you said, it belonged to J.D." She wiped her eyes again. "I was just using it. You can't prove that I ever had it."

"They already know about the phone, Debbie." I tried my most reasonable voice. "It would be better for you if you just took it to them voluntarily."

"Look, Jenna, don't you see? They're getting ready to arrest Lisa. This will just be the last nail in her coffin." She looked at me. "But what if she didn't find out about me and J.D.? What if she didn't kill him?"

"John will find out." I sounded confident, but I couldn't help remembering how I felt when Zac was a murder suspect. Even though I knew John was conscientious and did his best, I also knew he hadn't had all that much experience with murder.

"As long as they don't have this phone, they'll keep looking. If they have it, they'll just say, 'Here's our proof. J.D. and Debbie were cheating behind Lisa's back, so she killed him.' They won't look for anybody else." She sniffed. "If you give them the phone, what are they gonna do? Arrest her immediately. That's what. Put her in jail and throw away the key. Is that what you want?"

"No. Of course not." She might be right. Lisa could end up in jail. And unless they found another suspect, she could go to trial. Especially if there was a bloody towel in her car.

Debbie interrupted that awful thought. "Why don't you go talk to Lisa? Try to find out if she knew about us. If she didn't know, then the phone doesn't matter. If she did know, then take the phone to John." Now Debbie was the one using her most reasonable voice.

Just what I wanted to do. Confront yet another person who might be a murderer. "I guess I could at least go see her. But if I can tell she knows about you and J.D., I'll have to take the phone to John. And even if she doesn't, I think one of us will have to take it anyway."

"Just wait and see what she says," Debbie pleaded.

I turned the phone off and slipped it back into my pocket. It didn't look like I'd be getting rid of it today. But I knew someone would have to take it to John. And soon.

"Well, from what you told me about Jolene," Carly said, as we lazily paddled around the lake using foot-power, "Debbie's more J.D.'s type than Lisa is." She neatly turned our paddleboat away from a collision course with the twins.

I smiled as I cycled with my feet, too. "Wait until you meet Jolene. She makes Debbie look like Princess Di. But you're right. Of the two, Debbie is more like Jolene than Lisa is."

"So why didn't he just tell Lisa?"

I shrugged. "Maybe he just wanted to have Debbie as insurance in case things didn't work out. Debbie said they 'told themselves they were just friends.' So technically, they weren't dating. Maybe J.D. was just keeping his options open. And I'm sure he didn't want to lose his job."

"Or maybe he had planned to manipulate the situation in some way but died before he could," Carly mused.

Before I could answer, cold water sprayed us.

"Whooo!" Carly rubbed her hand across her face. "You sneaky girls splashed us on purpose!" Our blue and white paddleboat rocked as we turned and pedaled furiously to try and catch the twins.

"Y'all looked like you needed to have a little fun," Hayley called, grinning over her shoulder at us. "Hurry, Rachel, they're gaining!"

"I'm going as fast as I can," Rachel yelled.

"We're getting too old for this." Panting, Carly looked over at me and grinned. "Besides, they're lighter. They can go faster."

"No kidding." My muscles burned as I pedaled harder. "Youth wins again," I declared dramatically as the twins beat us by inches to the dock, our finish line.

"No more splashing us," Carly told the giggling girls. "Let's just relax and paddle around for a while. That way I may be able to catch my breath."

As the girls paddled their boat across the lake, Carly and I leaned back against our seats and tried to slow our pounding heartbeats. Carly kept an eye on the girls' boat as we talked.

"I can't even imagine what it would be like if something happened to one of them." She nodded toward the twins. "Poor Harvey and Alice."

"Yeah. I feel so sorry for them. I wish we knew exactly what happened." I leaned back and stuck my hand into the cool water. "I hate it that Marge didn't tell me not to mention J.D. to them." I trickled water down my sweaty face. "And Marge won't tell me anything else."

"Did you ask Mama?" Carly fanned herself with her hand. "She would know."

"No." I filled her in on Mama's plea for me to stay out of this case. "So I'm trying to keep a low profile." I relaxed against my seat. "Besides, I need an unbiased report."

"I think most of the people involved are pretty biased," Carly said dryly. "Too bad we can't just google it. But I'm pretty sure something that old won't be on the Internet."

"The archive room at the newspaper!" I turned to Carly. "As soon as we can, we need to go to the *Monitor* office. All we have to do is find the paper with the article in it." I didn't mention that there were forty years of papers to go through. No need to scare her off before we even got started.

"Sounds easy enough." Carly guided us up to the dock. We levered ourselves out of the boat and motioned for the girls to come on in.

While we were waiting for them to get out of their boat and join us, Daddy came toward us with fishing poles in one hand

and his tackle box in the other.

"Is it okay with you if the girls and I fish for a while?"

Carly nodded. "Jenna and I need to run an errand, anyway."

Daddy offered the poles to the giggling twins. "Let's see if we can catch some supper."

I glanced at the watch on Daddy's wrist. It was a little after five. Most of the *Monitor* employees should be gone. "Can the girls stay with you until we get back?"

"Of course they can. We may be out here an hour or more, anyway." Daddy rigged a pole for each of the girls, and they sat on the dock with their legs hanging off. "We'll take our catch up to the house when we finish."

"Pretty sure we'll catch some, aren't you, Grandpa?" Rachel said sassily.

"He knows *I* will," Hayley spouted off.

Daddy laughed, and Carly and I exchanged a grin. "They're growing up," she murmured. "Before I know it, they'll be grown and gone."

I stared at her as we climbed into my vehicle. "Are you okay?"

She nodded and stared out the window at the lake. "Just realizing how quickly things can change."

I frowned but concentrated on pulling onto the highway. Was Travis about to come barreling back into our lives? I wanted to ask. But I'd promised myself I'd wait until she got ready to tell me. And I would.

The parking area behind the newspaper office was empty when Carly and I pulled in.

"I'm glad no one is here. I'd rather not have to explain what we're looking for to anyone." I unlocked the door. "Even Tiffany."

I flipped the light switch on in the archive room, and Carly gasped. "Just find the paper with the article in it? I think this may be harder than I thought."

I explained that they were in order by date and that Marge had given me the month and year. So after narrowing our search to that one small area, we began to read.

After about fifteen minutes, I slapped the table. "Pay dirt!" I read the headline aloud to Carly. "LOCAL TEEN KILLED IN DRAG RACING ACCIDENT."

"Drag racing? No one mentioned that, did they?"

I shook my head and continued reading. " 'Fifteen-year-old Sara Coleman, daughter of Harvey and Alice Coleman, was the

204

victim of a fatal automobile accident. Coleman was a passenger in the car driven by Jimmy Finley, age seventeen, of Lake View. Witnesses said Finley lost control of the car when it hit a bump in the road while traveling at a high rate of speed. It then went airborne and flipped several times before landing in a ditch. Finley reported only minor injuries. Police have not yet determined whether alcohol or drugs were involved. The accident occurred off County Road 44.' "

"Wow," Carly said. "I'd envisioned something like a hit-and-run or maybe he was drunk and hit her car."

I laid the newspaper to the side. "So she chose to be there." I mulled that over for a few minutes.

"That probably makes it worse for her parents," Carly pointed out. "If she were a totally innocent victim, it may have been easier on them."

"I wonder if he was her boyfriend." I set the newspaper in its place. "Or if she did it on a dare."

"Maybe she just loved to go fast," Carly said.

We found another article dated two weeks later. The headline read, LOCAL TEEN PLEADS GUILTY IN FATAL ACCIDENT. I read the article aloud. " 'Jimmy Dean Finley pleaded guilty to vehicular homicide in Lake View District Court on Thursday. According to police, Finley and passenger, Sara Coleman, were involved in a high-speed drag race, when Finley lost control of his car, which went airborne. Miss Coleman was thrown from the car and killed instantly. Alcohol was a factor.' "

"Do you think there are any other articles about this?" I glanced at Carly.

"We're almost finished with the month. Let's go on and look through the rest of these."

A few minutes later, Carly said, "Oh, here's one!" She started reading. " 'PARENTS OF DEAD TEEN SUE PROPERTY OWNERS WHERE ACCIDENT OCCURRED. Harvey and Alice Coleman filed a wrongful death lawsuit against Bob and Wilma Pryor after the death of their daughter, Sara Coleman.' "

She stopped. "Bob and Wilma? What in the world?"

"Keep reading," I urged.

"The lawsuit alleges that the Pryors knowingly provided alcohol to minors while on their property."

I gasped. "I don't believe it."

She glanced back at the article. "Believe

it. Listen to this: 'According to unnamed sources, there have been numerous complaints from other parents about underage drinking and drag racing on the Pryors' property.' "

We looked at each other. "There has to be more. At least the trials of J.D. and of Bob and Wilma," Carly said.

I nodded. "And I have to see how they came out."

We began looking through the newspapers for the next month. But it wasn't until December that we scored.

" 'J.D. Finley has been sentenced to a year in juvenile detention,' " Carly read aloud.

A minute later I found the rest of the story. " 'Local residents Harvey and Alice Coleman have dropped their wrongful death suit against Bob and Wilma Pryor.' "

"Hank kept those last two uncharacteristically short, didn't he?" Carly said.

I nodded. "Marge said she begged him not to print anything at all. I suppose he just put what he felt his journalistic ethics required."

"So that's why Bob gave up the hippie life. . . ." Carly carefully put the newspaper back where it belonged. "And why everyone is suddenly remembering the past."

I nodded. "The question is, did someone

remember the past vividly enough to kill because of it?"

13

Never miss a good chance to shut up.

"Miss Jenna." Vini gave me a serious look. "If that woman comes in and pinches my jaw again, I will have to look for another job. Miss Carly will fire me, because I will be rude to a customer."

"Tell you what, Vini. I'll be on the lookout. When Jolene comes in, I'll be sure Harvey seats her in my section. Deal?"

"Thank you. Yes, it is a deal."

Consequently, when Jolene made an appearance toward the end of the noon rush, Harvey seated her at a table in the corner, and I took her order.

"I must be getting back to my roots or something," she commented as I set her sweet tea on the table. "I had that all the time when I was at my gramma's when I was a kid."

"If you don't mind my asking, where are

you from? Sometimes you sound like you're from Mississippi, and sometimes from New York or somewhere up there."

"Keeps you guessin', don't it?" She winked. "Actually, you ain't far off. I spent the summers in Texas with my gramma, but my folks lived in New Jersey. Then when I was old enough to make my own way, I went wherever the spirit moved me, from Florida to California and points in between. My trusty Mustang takes me wherever the good times are. I usually find me somebody to hang out with for a while, and then I move on. I'm a pretty good waitress, so I can work about anywheres."

I eyed her short, low-cut dress and stiletto heels, trying to picture Carly hiring her to work at the Down Home Diner. Nope. Couldn't see it.

"Now, let's get down to business. We've gotta hit the funeral parlor and figure out how much a buryin' is gonna set me back. Once me and the mortician come to terms, we need to set a date and get this thing done. I ain't one for havin' a long drawn-out grieving. Jimmy's dead. Let's get him in the ground and get on with life."

Once again, I found myself riding shotgun in the red Mustang. We pulled into the drive of the local funeral home and got out. Jolene checked to make sure her dress wasn't hitched up — or maybe to make sure it was. Then she pranced on her tall, thin heels into the building. I almost ran to keep up. I wanted a glimpse of Tom LeMay's face when he saw her. The plump, bald, middle-aged man met us at the door but took Jolene's appearance in stride.

"May I help you ladies?" His voice was calm and courteous.

"You betcha boots," Jolene answered. "We wanta bury a guy. What's the cheapest funeral we can have in this fancy place?"

Tom looked at me, and my face turned red. I fought the urge to turn and walk out as if I'd never seen Jolene before. Instead, I shrugged slightly and introduced her.

"I got a paper right here that says I'm the executor of Jimmy's will, so I got to do my duty and see him in the ground. I want it done decent, but I don't want to be ripped off, neither. You understand?" She wagged a pointed red fingernail under Tom's chin.

"Yes, ma'am. We aren't in the habit of ripping people off. Now, if you will follow me, I will show you our selection of caskets." He turned, and we followed.

An hour later, we emerged. Jolene was torn between exhilaration and gloom, because even though she'd talked Tom down on the price of his cheapest casket, the funeral was still going to "eat a hole" in her inheritance.

"But that's okay," she assured me. "Jimmy had a big wad in his bank account, and it's all mine. Whoo . . ." She shook her head. "It just goes to show. I never dreamed I'd be an heiress. I may just have to help them rube cops find the killer."

"Speaking of killers, have you thought any more about why someone might have shot J.D.?" I hated to question her outside the funeral home, but I needed to know. "I mean, what was he like? Did he leave enemies everywhere he went? We have very few murders here in our small town. And with him not being from here, I wondered if maybe he brought his killer with him, so to speak."

"Well, honey, if you're hintin' I offed him, you can get over it. I didn't even know where he was till that lawyer dude called me. And he said he had a whale of a job locatin' me."

"I didn't mean to imply anything about you, Jolene. Sorry if it sounded that way." She looked menacing when she was angry, though. I could imagine that snake tattoo shooting its fangs out at me. I hurried to soothe her. "I just thought you might give me some insight into J.D.'s character. But you don't have to."

"That's okay. I fly off the handle a little fast sometimes. Jumpin' to conclusions and missin' as my old gramma used to say." She sent me a forgiving grin. She mused for a minute then continued, "Wonder when Jimmy took to callin' hisself 'J.D.' Sounds right fancy, don't it?"

"I guess."

She ignored my answer. "Now that I think about it, he did make a few folks mad. You know, my best girlfriend back then — Melody was her name — she married herself a rich old man. Took her forever to find one, but she did." She shook her head in wonder. "He was an old coot — bald-headed and didn't have his own teeth. But he was loaded. That's the best kind of man, you know." Wink, wink.

"Well, I —"

She cut off any Dear Pru advice I might impart with a wave of her hand. "So, one night Melody and me have a girls' night out, and we meet this guy, a real hunk. I don't know how she does it, but before the night's over, she gets him to give her his number. The rest of the night, she's all braggin', you know, how she could pick up men without even tryin'. I kinda lost my cool and blubbered to Jimmy, wantin' him to tell me I was prettier'n Melody — which I was — but the next thing I know, he's callin' her and threatening to blab to her husband if she don't let him borrow her fancy car."

"So she was mad at him?"

"I'll say she was. Mad at both of us. Even though I was innocent as a newborn baby. She wouldn't speak to me for a long time. In fact, as long as Jimmy and me was together. She come around after I showed him the door, though. Should we put an obituary in the paper? Sort of let folks hereabouts know when the funeral is?" she asked without ever taking an audible breath.

"I'll take care of it. The editor and I are friends," I answered.

"I knew you was the right gal to take up with soon as I laid eyes on you." She slapped me on the back. Not lightly. She dropped me off at the diner, and I left her to her Mustang and musings and went home to get ready for work at the health club. On the way, I called Marge at the *Monitor,* and together we came up with an obituary for Jimmy Dean Finley.

I stuck my head into Bob's office. "If it's okay with you, I'm going to come by tomorrow night for a couple of hours and see what all needs to be done." I thought it might be easier if I had some time by myself to get reacquainted with the running of a health club.

"Sounds good. Let me get you a key." He motioned me to come inside. "Got a minute?" He made a pushing motion toward the door, so I shut it.

Poor Bob. He'd aged so much in the last few days. "Of course." I sat down. And tried not to think of how often I had dreamed of owning this place. And how aggravated I'd been at Bob and Lisa when I quit. Time to put those thoughts behind me.

He pushed the key across the desk toward me. "I guess you heard that they may arrest Lisa any minute now. I know it's the talk of the town." His shoulders slumped as if the weight of the world rested on them.

I nodded.

Bob leaned forward. "I think she's being framed, Jenna." He lowered his voice. "Some stuff happened a long time ago. And ever since, Harvey has hated me. Remember how he and Hank Templeton teamed up on the zoning board to keep my business outside of town? I think he did this just to get back at me."

"Killed an innocent person just to get revenge on you, Bob?" I wondered if self-

215

centeredness was an inherited trait.

"No . . ." Bob suddenly looked very uncomfortable, as if he hadn't thought this far ahead.

I considered telling him I already knew, but I couldn't think of a tactful way.

"The thing is . . . J.D. was involved back then, too. In the stuff that happened. So Harvey hated us both. This way he killed two birds with one stone." He studied the framed picture of Lisa and Fluffy. "Killing J.D. and setting Lisa up for it settles the score with both of us."

I nodded. In some twisted way, I could see his logic. If Lisa were found guilty, it would be worse for Bob than if he himself were sent to prison.

"You know, don't you?"

I looked up into Bob's questioning eyes. I didn't see any reason to deny it. "How could you tell?"

"I'd braced myself for your questions. I knew as soon as I hinted at the past, you'd want to know it all. But you didn't ask me anything."

"I just didn't want to make it any harder for you than it is already," I said quietly.

He spun his chair around, turning his back to me. When I heard his voice, thick with tears, I knew why. "Wilma and I, we'd just moved here from California not long before all that. She wanted to settle down, but I liked the fact that the kids all thought I was cool." His voice broke. "They made me feel young. I didn't see any harm in it."

I stared at his shaking shoulders.

He shook his head and didn't speak for a minute. Even from the back, I could see he was struggling to keep any composure at all.

"We didn't know about the drag racing, but if I could go back and live that part of my life over, I would. We both told Harvey and Alice how sorry we were. And they seemed to forgive us to some extent. Dropped the suit, which you probably know. But when Lisa was born a couple of years later, all the old feelings of hate boiled up again. They both looked at us like we had no right to have a daughter when they'd lost theirs because of my stupidity."

"So now you think Harvey wants to take your daughter away from you?"

He nodded, with his back still toward me.

"Does Lisa know about this?"

"No!"

"J.D. didn't tell her?"

"No. He probably would've. But he died before he got a chance."

My heart thudded in my chest.

He spun around to face me, mindless now of the tears coursing down his cheeks. "I didn't mean it like that. I didn't kill him."

"So he wasn't blackmailing you?"

"Not really. He just kept reminding me that he had one over on me."

The precursor to blackmail. Reason enough to murder someone? Maybe. But I didn't believe for a minute Bob would kill someone and let his precious daughter take the blame. In my eyes, that fact alone exonerated him.

I stood and put the key in my pocket. "I'm sorry."

He nodded. "Me, too."

I left him to his thoughts.

On the way home, I stopped by Carly's to tell her what Bob said about Harvey being the killer.

"You know, as bad as I hate to say this, the same things could be said of Alice," she said.

"Alice? You're just mad because she bosses you around in the kitchen," I teased her. "*And* she makes better pies."

"Ha. She does not make better pies. She just has more years of practice." Carly fluffed her short curls. "Just wait until you taste the pies I make when I get as old as she is."

"You're right, though. She does have the same motive."

"But not the same opportunity," Carly said suddenly. "Because Harvey took the trash out."

I put my hand to my mouth. "You're right. He could have shot J.D. then walked right back into the diner."

"He would have stayed out there long enough to see you and knock you in the head. But as busy as we were . . ."

I remembered how long it took anyone to realize I was hurt. "Nobody even would have noticed."

14

You catch more flies with honey
than you do with vinegar.

"Jen?" Carly sounded harried on the phone.
"I have a huge favor to ask."

"Let's hear it."

"Is there any chance you're going out to
the athletic club tonight?"

"I was planning on it. Why?"

"The girls and I need a ride to school."

"No problem." The school was out near
Bob's gym anyway. "Is your car torn up?"

Silence.

"Carly, you still there?"

"I'm here," she said, embarrassment
evident in her tone. "Technically, my car
isn't 'torn up.' It's more like 'out of gas.' "

Any other time, she'd have called Elliott
to bring her some gas or give her a ride to
school. I certainly wasn't complaining, but
it made me sad to see them drifting apart.

"I'll be right over."

When I pulled up in front of their cabin, Carly and the girls came running out and jumped in.

"How long will your school thing last?" I asked when we got on the road.

"It's an open house," Rachel said from the backseat.

"So there's no set ending time," Hayley finished.

I glanced at Carly. "In that case, why don't you just drop me off at the gym, and I'll work until you pick me back up?"

"Really? That would be perfect. You're a lifesaver."

"That's better than a Dum Dum, I guess." I tossed her a silly smile.

The girls giggled and Carly groaned. "That was corny, even for you."

"Yes, well, I'm getting cornier in my old age."

"You only use that term because you know I'll always be older than you," she said.

"You're probably right." I swung the car into the almost-deserted parking lot of the Lake View Athletic Club and jumped out.

Carly jumped out, too, and ran around to the driver's seat. She gave me a quick hug before sliding in. "Bye, Jenna, and thanks again."

She waited to make sure I was inside before leaving the club parking lot. Ordinarily I would think that was overkill, but with a real killer on the loose, I wasn't complaining. The thought of a "real killer" sent a shiver down my spine and made me glad to hear the hum of voices in the exercise room.

I shivered again when I started looking at the mess that Lisa had left. Her housekeeping skills were on par with her management skills — although I had a feeling it was more of an "I don't care" attitude than not being *able* to do it.

After I'd been cleaning for a while, Dave stuck his head in the door. "I'm about to lock up. You want me to wait for you?"

"No, thanks. I've still got a little more to do here."

He nodded. "Rumor has it there's a ghost in here late at night, so if you hear anything, get your cell phone ready to take a pic."

"If I saw a ghost, the last thing I'd be worried about would be taking its picture."

He shrugged. "Your loss. A photo of a real ghost would sell for no telling how much."

"I'd rather just have peace and quiet and get my job done. But thanks." I glanced back at the stack of junk I was sorting through then thought of something. "Oh, and Dave . . ."

He stuck his head back in the door. "Yeah?"

"Thanks for spooking me before I get locked in here by myself."

"Spook the legendary Jenna Stafford? No way."

He laughed all the way down the hall. I threw myself back into cleaning. I should have turned some music on, because as soon as I knew he was gone, I started hearing little noises. Creaking noises, swishing noises, ceiling fan noises.

A scraping sound from the back door might as well have been a cannon shot. That's the kind of noise that puts all other noises to shame. The kind you can't ignore or explain away. That was definitely something. I cautiously peeped over the top of the cabinet I didn't realize I'd ducked behind.

I heard footsteps, and they were coming this way. No way anyone would have any business in the back room of the club after hours. Well, no one but a cleaning freak like me. Unfortunately, the cabinet was too small for me to crawl into. I wished I'd closed the hall door when I came in here, but all I'd had on my mind was getting the place aired out and cleaned up.

Suddenly, it hit me. Mama had been wrong. All those times she'd warned me about curiosity leading to an unhappy ending for me, she should have told me that cleaning would be the death of me. That would have saved me a lot of prune hands and sore knees over the years. And tonight it might have saved my life.

The footsteps stopped at the door. I wondered if my foot was sticking out beyond the edge of the cabinet. If I drew it in, would it make noise? Speaking of noise, was that whistling? A whistling killer? "Yankee Doodle," no less. Forget my whole death-by-cleaning theory. Mama was right, as usual. Curiosity would kill me. But I had to look. I borrowed a trick from Tiffany and prayed that my "hand" gun would be as unnecessary as hers had been.

I swung out from behind the cabinet in one fluid motion, bringing my fake gun out in front of me. "Who's there?" I said in my most commanding voice to the shadow in the hallway.

"It is Vini! Who is there?" His voice trembled.

My taut muscles went limp. "It's Jenna."

He stuck his head inside the doorway, and his eyes widened. "What are you doing here?"

"I think that's my line. I work here." I frowned. "If I remember correctly, you don't."

"I can explain." He walked into the room, his face suffused with color. "Or I could, but I do not want to get someone into trouble."

I crossed my arms in front of me. "Well, 'someone' *is* in trouble. It's you. So you'd better start explaining." I was still shaky from the fright he'd given me, which made me sound tougher than I felt. "You came in the back door. Did you break the lock?"

"No." Vini sounded shocked at the idea. "I did not break it. That would be wrong."

"Then how did you get in?"

"I used the key." He dangled a key in front of my face. I snatched it from his hand.

"*Where* did you get this key?" I demanded.

"W–well." He backed up as if he still believed I had a gun. "I — I will tell you."

"Yes. You certainly will tell me."

"Promise not to get her into trouble," he said.

"I can't make any promises until I know the whole story."

He gave it serious consideration then sent me a tentative smile. "I trust you."

I was pretty sure I knew by now who had given him the key. "Sorry I was so sharp with you, but you scared me to death."

"I did not know you were here. I would have been quieter."

"Don't worry about it. Just tell me why you're here."

"I live here."

I'd thought the shock of him walking in on me had been the biggest shock of the night, but I was obviously wrong.

"Vini, you can't live here. This isn't a house. It's not even an apartment."

"Believe me, it is only temporary," he insisted. "The people I lived with — they got transferred and had to move. I had no place to sleep. I could not stay at the college because I did not sign up for a dormitory room. Besides, the dormitory costs more than I can afford."

"So Gail gave you a key and said you could stay here for a while?"

"Yes. You guessed it." He nodded. "She has been very kind to me. She would let me stay at her apartment. But it would not look good."

"So you've been living here for a while?"

"I was sleeping in my van and taking showers here when I worked here. But after I got fired, Gail said I could stay if I didn't tell anyone." His forehead wrinkled. "I hope she is not mad at me. She told me to only come in the back door when the club is empty." He gave me a reproachful look. "No car is out there tonight. So I thought it was empty. You scared me."

"Vini, you can't stay here anymore."

His shoulders slumped in defeat. "Are you going to tell on Gail?"

Bob had enough on his mind. And Vini staying here hadn't hurt anything, really. "I'm not sure. Not right now."

"So I will move my things back out to my van." He turned and walked away.

When he was gone, I picked up my cell phone and made a quick call. "Mama, I know it's late, but I need to rent a cabin for the night." I quickly explained the situation to her.

"We have a couple of empty cabins he can choose from, but you won't be paying," she said firmly.

"Just for tonight," I agreed. "Then we'll figure something out."

The next morning, I hurried over to Stafford Cabins as soon as I knew Mama and Daddy would have the office opened.

The front office was deserted when I walked in.

"Good morning," Daddy called. "We're in the back."

I stepped down the tiny hall to the little break area Mama had fixed up. They were sitting at the table drinking coffee. And holding hands.

I blushed. Would Alex and I still be that much in love after that many years? I had a feeling we would. He was due back from the conference on Saturday. I made a mental note to call him later and tell him how much I looked forward to growing old with him. That done, I turned my attention back to my parents. "You really shouldn't just call out for anyone to come on back," I scolded. "I could have been an ax murderer."

"I suppose you could have," Daddy said thoughtfully, looking at Mama. "But I thought we raised her better than that, didn't you, Elizabeth?"

Mama nodded, never missing a beat. "Of course, if you were an ax murderer, dear . . . it really wouldn't matter whether we invited you in or not, would it?"

I sighed. "Never mind."

"Tell us about Vini."

"Yes. He was up at dawn, sweeping the office porch and straightening the deck chairs," Daddy said.

I smiled, because I could see him doing that. "Well, you know, he came here as an exchange student in high school then managed to get his paperwork to stay on for college. With a limited work visa, he's living on very little money. He was living with a sponsor family, but the husband was transferred to Little Rock, which left Vini homeless."

"Oh my. Bless his heart," Mama said.

I nodded. "He's been sleeping at the club and just eating what he gets at the diner. But he needs a place where he can study and relax." I looked at them and chose my words carefully. I wanted to be sure they knew that helping Vini was something I wanted to do. Not something I wanted them to do.

They were staring at each other without speaking. It was one of those looks that made me feel as if there was a conversation going on that I wasn't a part of.

I continued, "I was thinking that maybe I could pay a reduced fee for one of the cabins. I know you sometimes do a weekly rate, and I've even seen you offer a monthly rate to a few —"

"Hush, dear, so we can think," Mama said sweetly.

I hushed.

"Are you thinking what I'm thinking?" she asked Daddy, her eyes sparkling.

He nodded. "It's an answer to a prayer.

Cabin 40."

I just stared at them. "We don't have forty cabins."

Mama laughed. "You remember cabin 40. We named it that because it's out in the back forty." She sipped her coffee and grinned at my still puzzled expression. "In other words, it's so far from the office we got more complaints than it was worth. So when a storm blew a tree across the porch a couple of years ago, we just moved the tree and closed the cabin."

Daddy picked up the story. "We were just talking yesterday about what we were going to do with it. There was some damage to the porch, but the cabin is livable. We can have power hooked back up with no trouble. To pay for his keep, Vini can clean it and work on the porch as he has time. After he finishes that, if he still needs a place to live, we've got plenty of other jobs that need doing."

I frowned. "So you really do want the cabin fixed up?"

Mama nodded. "We've tried to figure out what to do with it."

"It was sweet of you to want to help him, honey," Daddy said. "But a man needs to earn his own way when he can. Keeps his character strong."

"A hand up is much better than a hand-out," Mama agreed.

I smiled at them and gave them each a hug. "I'll go tell Vini the great news."

I didn't have to be at work at the athletic club until three, so after I made Vini's day, I decided I would do what I had promised Debbie and go visit Lisa at Bob and Wilma's.

I pulled into the circular driveway in front of the elegant split-level glass and cedar house. Wilma answered the doorbell. She seemed genuinely happy to see me. When I told her why I was there, she ushered me up the wide oak stairway and to Lisa's barely opened bedroom door. I turned to ask Wilma if she wanted to go in and tell Lisa I was there. But before I could say a word, she'd retreated down the stairs.

I tapped on the door, and it opened under my knuckles. My guess was that the room hadn't changed since Lisa was a little girl. A pink ruffled bedspread covered the bed underneath the white canopy. It made me think of Barbie's bedroom. And there was Barbie, um, Lisa, in bed propped up on some pillows, a romance novel in her hand.

"Hey," I said, giving her my best smile. "How are you?"

"How do you think I am?" she grumbled.

"Upset, I imagine." I nodded toward the closed blinds behind the frilly curtains. "Would you like me to open the blinds and let some sunshine in?" I took a step toward the window, and a tiny white fur ball came alive on the bed. Teeth bared and growling, Fluffy didn't want me close to her mistress.

I froze then took a step back. The dog retreated to its pillow but kept its eyes focused on me.

"No, I don't need sunshine." Lisa ignored Fluffy and glared at me. "I just lost a, well, a very good friend. In a brutal way. And now the police think I killed him. I'll be lucky if I don't get arrested before I can even attend his funeral tomorrow." She pinched her lips together. "And I never looked good in orange." She was probably right; apparently pink was more her color. "So, yes, I'm a bit upset. I think that's understandable."

"It definitely is understandable. But maybe if you got up and went to the gym, you'd feel better. Sometimes getting that adrenaline pumping —"

She pushed herself up in the bed. "I'm sure you came to interrogate me about something, so why don't you just get on with it?"

My eyes widened. "I came to check on you. People are worried about you."

"Like who?"

"Like Debbie."

I watched her face, but she had no visible reaction to Debbie's name. So I forged on. "You and Debbie met J.D. at the same time, right?"

"Yes, so?"

"What did Debbie think about him?"

"She thought what every woman who met him thought — that he was hot. And she was right."

"Do you think she was put out that he chose you instead of her? I mean, y'all met him at the same time, you both thought he was attractive, but he chose you."

"Well, come on. I mean, I love Debbie and all, but look at her and look at me. Can you see any guy choosing her when I'm available?" She smirked. "No. J.D. was mine for as long as I wanted him. I just had to decide whether I wanted him or if I was going back to Larry."

She really was totally self-centered. "Speaking of Larry," I said. I sort of felt odd calling him Larry. I'd always hear him referred to as Lawrence, but Bob and Lisa both called him Larry, so I decided to follow their example. "How did he feel about you and J.D.?"

"Poor Larry." Lisa lost some of her composure. "That's my biggest fear." She swiped at a tear. It even looked real. Maybe there was a heart in there somewhere. "He was so jealous. What if he decided to have it out with J.D. and just lost control? I don't think I could bear to be the wife of a murderer." She shivered and continued. "Besides, if Larry killed J.D., it was partly my fault. He was always possessive. That's one reason I left him. I just had to have some breathing room."

"Oh. I thought —" I came to a stop.

"You thought what?" Comprehension washed over her face. "Ooh. Dad told you that story I told him. About how Larry was abusive. Well, I had to say something. Dad adores me. But he expects me to stay married unless I have a good reason not to. So I gave him a good reason." She shrugged.

I just shook my head. This girl was the queen of situation ethics.

"I'm curious about something." I hadn't planned to ask this question, but now that I was here, I had to know.

"What about?"

"Rumor has it that there was a towel under your car seat with J.D.'s blood on it. Do you know how it got there?"

She frowned. "I heard that, too, but I had no idea it was there."

"Wonder how it got there?"

"Well, Sherlock, I suppose it had to be either one of two things. Either J.D. cut himself shaving or something and stuffed the towel under there himself. Or someone planted it."

I ignored her "Sherlock" dig in favor of getting information. "Which do you think happened?"

She shrugged. "Since someone stole my gun, my guess is the same person planted the towel in my car. I just can't figure out who would want to hurt me like that." She reached over and rubbed Fluffy's head. "Or hurt my precious baby, either."

"They hurt your dog?" I asked, eyeing the tiny ball of fluff. Other than occasionally baring its teeth, it looked fine to me.

She put her hands over the dog's ears. "Fluffy's not just a dog. She's my baby." I was wrong. Lisa wasn't totally self-centered. After all, she had spared a thought for her "baby." "And if I'm upset, she gets upset."

"I understand." I had a neurotic cat, didn't I? "Some animals are sensitive to their master's moods." And I'm sure if any animal was sensitive, it would be Fluffy. And Lisa probably had more moods than most.

"I think I'll call Dad and have him take Fluffy out to Larry. He's the only person who loves her as much as I do."

Just one more errand for poor Bob to do for his princess. On the other hand, this would be a perfect opportunity for me to check out Larry in person. "Or I can run Fluffy out to Larry's."

"Oh." She gave me a measured look. "I suppose that would work."

Talk about gratitude. Not that I expected any.

She called Larry and told him I was coming then gave me directions and stressed that Fluffy only traveled in a cage. At least she got out of bed long enough to get all of the dog's things together. She actually packed a suitcase for the canine.

I lugged the suitcase to my car first then came back for the dog.

"Remind Larry this is only temporary," she told me. "As soon as this mess is behind me, I get her back."

"I'll tell him," I promised.

I was almost to the top of the stairs when Lisa called me back. And to think I'd thought my days of being summoned by her were over when I quit the club. "Yes?" I said. I lugged the small dog carrier back up to her room.

She looked up from her novel as if I were bothering her. "Oh. I wanted to ask you something. I don't usually listen to rumors, but I heard J.D.'s ex-wife was in town. They say she's really trashy. Is that true?"

I stared at her. I was taking her dog to her husband until she could get over her boy-friend's murder. And she was asking me if someone else was "trashy." "You'd have to be your own judge of that, Lisa," I said softly and let myself out the door.

"I'll see for myself at the funeral tomor-row anyway," she called haughtily as I walked down the stairs.

Fluffy, in the carrier by my side, barked in reply. But I just kept walking.

15

Better than a poke in the eye
with a sharp stick

"How do you talk me into these things?" Carly settled into her seat and buckled in.

"You mean you don't enjoy going with me to confront possible murderers?"

"Don't act so surprised," she drawled. "I told you the first time you dragged me into trying to solve a murder that I'm a big chicken."

"Well, now that we know he didn't abuse Lisa, what do you think the chances are that Larry did it?" I asked.

"You said he's really jealous, so I'm not sure." She glanced at Fluffy in her carrier in the backseat. "I guess it all depends on how he treats the dog."

I grinned as I guided the car into the fringes of Lake View's ritziest neighborhood. "So murderers are mean to animals as a general rule?"

"Probably. You're the expert on murder, not me."

I turned into a private drive and drove through the imposing gates and up a long driveway to an even more impressive house.

We sat for a second rubbernecking at the mansion on the hill. "Doesn't that just make you want to call the butler to bring high tea, dahling?" My English accent was atrocious, flavored as it was by an Arkansas drawl.

"Ignore her," Carly muttered to Fluffy as she got the carrier out of the backseat. "She gets goofier when she's nervous."

"She's the one you need to watch out for," I said to the dog. "She gets clumsy when she's nervous."

Carly snickered. "True."

In spite of our warnings to Fluffy, we made it to the front door without incident. When I pushed the doorbell, loud, rich chimes sounded inside.

A middle-aged woman wearing a white blouse tucked neatly in a knee-length black skirt opened the door. We told her our names, and she showed us to a spacious room with floor-to-ceiling bookshelves and a bay window complete with window seat. Fluffy jumped wildly in her carrier, making sharp yelping noises and scrabbling around. Carly handed me the plastic box, and I set it on the floor but left the door latched.

"Mr. Hall will be with you in a moment." She backed out and closed the double doors behind us. It occurred to me that was what they always meant in old books when they said someone withdrew.

"This must be the withdrawing room," I whispered to Carly. She looked at me as if I'd lost it. "Never mind," I muttered. Jokes that have to be explained are never funny.

Before we had time to get nosy, the double doors opened again. "Good afternoon." Lawrence Hall was a good twenty-five years Lisa's senior, but his white hair and sharp blue eyes gave him a distinguished man-about-town look. All smiles and gracious host, today he did remind me of Mr. Rourke from *Fantasy Island.*

"Ah, I see you've brought my baby home." He bent down toward the carrier where Fluffy was making happy squeaky noises. "Thank you." He opened the carrier and lifted Fluffy out. He was rewarded with a long pink tongue licking him all over the face.

While he was talking baby talk to Fluffy, Carly looked at me and shrugged. I knew she was remembering our conversation in the car about whether murderers were nice to animals.

Larry gave us a sheepish grin. "I've missed her."

I smiled. No kidding. We'd never have guessed.

He sat down in a leather recliner with Fluffy on his lap.

"Would you ladies care for some refreshment?" Without waiting for a reply, he rang a bell on the table beside his chair. The woman who had shown us in entered with a tray holding three glasses of iced tea and a plate of home-baked chocolate chip cookies.

Larry handed us each a glass of tea and held out the plate for us to get a napkin and a cookie.

"Thanks," we chorused.

"Nice weather for September, isn't it?" he said just as Carly and I bit into our cookies. I've always wondered why people offer someone food then immediately start a conversation.

We nodded.

He cleared his throat and tried again. "The Cardinals look like they might go all the way this year."

I took a sip of my tea. "If they can keep their offense hitting like they have the last few games, they definitely have a chance."

Larry's aristocratic eyebrows rose. "Ah, a fellow baseball fan."

"She went to St. Louis to a game the other night and sat eight rows behind home plate," Carly said.

Larry looked at me and nodded. "Nice seats . . . Sometimes I think we miss the feel of being a part of the crowd in our private box."

"Daddy always says if you can't smell the popcorn, you might as well be watching it on TV," I said without thinking.

And that was the end of the baseball conversation.

Carly and I exchanged a glance. I'd wanted to talk to Larry, but the atmosphere was so stilted that it was hard to ask questions like I usually did. I cleared my throat. "We'd better be going."

"Wait." Larry leaned forward and set his glass down. "How's Lisa?"

"She's having a pretty hard time."

"We all reap what we sow, don't we?" His voice was hard.

I winced. "Yes, I guess we do. But then again, we all make mistakes." I wasn't sure Lisa had hit rock bottom yet. And it obviously wouldn't hurt her to do some serious soul searching, but I still pitied her.

Larry rang the bell, and the maid appeared. "Please take Fluffy outside for a walk," he commanded.

The maid quickly took the little white dog and left the room.

Larry turned back to us and crossed his arms in front of his chest. "I offered to hire a lawyer for her, but she said Bob was taking care of it." A strange expression crossed his face. "Looks like she's going to need a good one."

"Do you think she killed him?" Carly asked, and he and I both looked at her in surprise. She shrugged. "You know her a lot better than we do."

He considered her question then shook his head slowly. "She's been tired of me for at least three years, and she didn't try to kill me. Why would she decide to murder to get rid of a boyfriend?" When he said the word "boyfriend," the veins in his neck stood out and his face grew red.

Thoughts of Debbie and her cell phone secret flitted through my mind. But after visiting Lisa, I was convinced that she didn't know about J.D. and Debbie. No one was that good an actress.

"But if she did have a strong motive, do you think she's capable of murder?" Carly persisted. I gave her a mental thumbs-up sign. Sometimes when I least expected it, her inner Nancy Drew kicked in. It always made me proud.

"Aren't we all capable of murder in the right circumstances?" Larry gave Carly an enigmatic smile.

She stiffened, and I waited for righteous indignation to spew forth. She surprised me.

"In what circumstance would you, for instance, be capable of murder?" She smiled sweetly at him, tilted her head to one side, and waited for an answer.

"Oh, I don't know. It would take more than my wife running off with a guy for me to kill him, if that's what you're getting at." And he smiled right back at her. "I might be tempted to kill *her* in that instance. But not him."

"And yet . . ."

"And yet, Lisa's not dead." He smiled. "It's all wrong, isn't it? Is that why you came out here? To ask me if I killed this guy?"

"Well." Following Carly's lead, I spoke more boldly than I normally would. "Do you have an alibi?"

"I don't need one. Unless you have a badge stashed somewhere on your person, and I don't think you do, I don't have to answer to you."

"So you refuse to say where you were the

night of the murder?"

"I refuse to answer impertinent questions from meddling women who should be minding their own business. There. Is that blunt enough for you?"

His chilly smile never faltered as he stood and gestured to the door.

"Ladies? Let me show you out. Thank you for bringing Fluffy. Give Lisa my regards." His voice hardened. "And tell her I won't wait forever for her to come to her senses. Good-bye, ladies." And with a mocking bow, he ushered us out the front door. It closed with a definite click.

"That went well," Carly commented wryly as we exited the gates and headed home.

"I hate funerals," I complained to Carly as I pulled on one black shoe and looked around for the other one. "If Jolene hadn't pressured me, I wouldn't go."

"Oh, who are you kidding?" Carly pitched me my other shoe from the closet. "I'm the one who should be complaining about being dragged along. You know what you always say about the murderer returning to the scene of the crime. You wouldn't miss this, and you know it."

I ducked my head. "You know me too well. But I do feel sorry for Jolene. She's kind of obnoxious, but she doesn't know anyone in town, and she was once married to J.D."

"I feel sorry for her, too, I guess. But I could do it from a distance. Especially since most of my employees seem to be taking off to go."

"Most of your employees? Who besides Debbie?" I gave her a sheepish grin. "And me?"

"Vini."

"Vini?" That was a surprise.

"Apparently Gail asked him to go with her. I think they kind of like each other, but they're both too busy or too shy to do much about it."

"Wonder why Gail is going?" I'd understood she hadn't been fond of J.D. when they worked together.

"Gail's a younger version of us, Jenna. Raised by a Southern mama to do the right thing whether you want to or not. He was a coworker, and it's the right thing to go to coworkers' funerals."

"I wonder if any of his grandmother's friends will be there."

"They might. But with all the trouble he apparently gave her, they might not."

"But he did come to her funeral," I reminded her.

"Yeah, probably just to see what he could get." Once again my sister sounded cynical. "Are you almost ready?"

"Yeah, Jolene wanted to pick us up here, but I convinced her to meet us at the funeral home. Wonder how Tom will do with the funeral?"

"Oh, I think he can handle it. Assuming no one gets shot." Carly referred to the last funeral we'd attended.

"Don't even think that!" I shuddered. "I just meant since he didn't know J.D. And since at least one current girlfriend, and possibly two, along with the ex-wife will probably all attend. It could be awkward."

"Or it could be illuminating. Maybe someone will confess to his murder."

I shook my head. "Somehow I doubt that."

As soon as Carly and I entered the funeral home chapel, Jolene strutted toward us. In deference to the solemn occasion, she had on her black halter today with a black leather skirt and black boots that came up over her knees. Her snake tattoo matched her eye liner perfectly.

"You've got to be kidding," Carly hissed in my ear from behind.

"Serious as a heart attack," I murmured. "Just wait." I'd tried to paint her a word picture of J.D.'s ex-wife, but obviously my description had fallen short of the reality.

I introduced the two women, and Carly expressed polite condolences.

Jolene slapped my arm with the back of her hand. "Girlfriend, didn't you tell your sister that dying was the best thing Jimmy Dean ever did for me?"

Carly's eyes widened, but she didn't say a word. She and Mama were both so blessed with knowing the right thing to say that I kind of felt better that Jolene left her speechless.

Tom LeMay, the funeral director, motioned Jolene toward the back. She waved at him and turned back to us. "When this is done, we need to go out and celebrate."

Again Carly didn't utter a word. Not even an "It was nice meeting you."

When Jolene was gone, we found a seat halfway down the aisle, and Carly suddenly rediscovered her voice. "I can't believe I let you talk me into this. That woman is crazy."

I shrugged. "She's odd. But she's honest. Sometimes that's refreshing."

Carly's face paled. "What do you mean by that?"

I frowned. "I don't mean anything by that. Why?"

Before she could answer, a stir at the back

of the small crowd drew our attention. Lisa, dressed in an elegant black dress and flanked by her parents, walked past Jolene as if she weren't there. Lisa held a dainty handkerchief to her eyes, but Bob and Wilma looked grimly forward. Each held one of Lisa's elbows, but she didn't look heartbroken enough to faint. In fact, either her mascara was very waterproof or the handkerchief was a show. I saw no tears. They took a seat across the aisle from us, but they didn't look our way.

A murmured conversation behind us caused me to look back just as Tiffany and Ricky slid into the pew behind us.

She leaned forward. "Hi." She spoke in the low tones people often adopt in funeral situations. "I don't usually cover funerals, but since this guy was murdered, I figured I might get a column out of it for the paper."

"I doubt there will be many people here," I responded.

"That's why I dragged Ricky along." She patted his hand tucked around her elbow. "I thought it'd look more respectful if there were a few people attending."

"I brought Carly for the same reason," I said.

Like Carly, Rick looked as if he'd rather

be anywhere but here, but he mustered a smile.

"Yep, that's me. The pew-filler," he muttered.

"It's so nice to have someone who doesn't mind giving up his free time when I need him." Tiffany gave Rick a dazzling smile.

Over Tiffany's shoulder, I saw Gail and Vini come in. Vini looked extremely uncomfortable and kept tugging at the tie wedged around his throat. Gail had the appearance of someone performing an unpleasant duty. She and Vini sat toward the back and spoke to each other in whispers without looking around at all.

An elderly couple entered next. They spoke briefly to Jolene and settled themselves directly in front of me. After a few moments of getting settled, the gray-haired woman turned around to me.

"Excuse me. Were you married to Jimmy? Someone said his wife was here."

"That woman at the back is his wife." Her husband nudged her and spoke loudly enough to be heard all over the building. "She told you that. You should've worn your hearing aid. Now turn around here and quit meddling."

I bit back a smile. Would that be Alex and me in forty years? I glanced at them again.

They looked vaguely familiar, and I was pretty sure they were the couple who talked loudly during the last funeral I attended.

"I was Mindy Finley's closest neighbor and best friend for thirty years. If I want to ask questions about her grandson, I will." She twisted back to face me. "I hadn't seen Jimmy since he was a kid. He used to stay with his grandma sometimes. He worried her to death with his constant shenanigans. She bailed him out time and time again until she had nothing left to give." She shook her head. "But he had the nerve to show up at her funeral looking for an inheritance. Now he's got himself killed."

Her husband tugged at her, and she turned around without waiting for any comments from me. Just as Tom started to escort Jolene to the front of the funeral parlor, the door opened and closed quickly and someone sat toward the back. I glanced around as discreetly as possible to see if I could spot the newcomers. Harvey and Alice. Came to make sure their nemesis was really gone, I guessed.

Across the way, and also on the back row, was a woman with a black dress, black hat, and glasses. I peered at her and nudged Carly. "You're right. Down Home's staff is almost all here. Debbie's even back there."

Carly nodded dully, and I turned my attention back to her. "Are you sick?"

She shook her head.

Before I could question her further, a loud *"Psst!"* brought my attention to the aisle.

Jolene had stopped right beside me with Tom LeMay still on her arm. She looked at me and motioned around the sparsely populated room. "So which one was J.D.'s girlfriend?"

Heat crept up my face. I glanced at the spectators, who were all watching me. Debbie had taken the sunglasses off and was staring at me, wide-eyed. Lisa glanced toward me then looked away. "The one in black," I whispered.

Before she could press me, Tom tugged gently on her arm. "Miss Highwater, we really must begin."

She waggled her fingers at me and walked to the front and sat down.

Without warning, "Born to Be Wild" blared from the speakers. Everyone jumped. Jolene had apparently done a little tweaking of the funeral plans that she and I had made together. When the song finished, a man in a black suit got up and read the obituary. Then he cleared his throat. For the next few minutes, he spoke in fairly generic terms about how quickly life passes by and how awful it is to waste it.

Even though I knew what he said was true, my mind started to inventory all the people who might have killed Jimmy Dean Finley, their motives, and their alibis. Beside me, I suddenly felt Carly shaking. I looked over and drew in a sharp breath. Tears were coursing down her face, and she was quietly sobbing. "Carly?" I whispered. "Are you hurting?"

She shook her head.

"Are you sick?" Sympathetic tears were pricking my own eyes, even though I couldn't imagine that we were crying about J.D.

Another shake of her head.

I handed her a couple of tissues from the box in the pew beside me and put my arm around her. "It's okay," I murmured, all thoughts of suspects and alibis vanquished from my mind. "What's wrong?" I tried one more time, but she shook her head yet again.

"I can't talk about it here," she whispered, each word punctuated by a quiet gulp.

"Then let's go somewhere where we can." I stood, helped her to her feet, and guided her to the back and out the double doors. No doubt we'd be the talk of the town, but I didn't care what people thought. The important thing was figuring out what was wrong with Carly.

Out in the courtyard, she quit trying to hold it in and started sobbing harder. My legs trembled as we sank onto a wrought-iron bench. "Car?" I wiped her curls back from her face. "Did you know J.D.?"

As she shook her head, relief coursed through me. Followed quickly by extreme confusion. "Why are we crying?"

"It's Travis," she choked out.

My heart jumped. Her ex-husband had been found. "He's here?"

She looked up at me, dark mascara tracks trailing down her cheeks. "Jenna. Travis is dead."

16

The hard thing about business is
mindin' your own.

"Oh no." I reached over and took Carly's
hand in mine.

"I'm sorry."

We sat there for a few minutes without
speaking, letting the cool breeze dry our
tears as they fell. My natural curiosity was
strangely dormant. A man I'd considered a
brother had lost his life. He'd lost any hope
of a second chance. Of reconciliation with
his children. Had it seemed worth it to him
after the initial infatuation was over? I guess
we'd never know. Nor did it really matter
now. Any lingering bitterness I had toward
the man who'd broken my sister's heart and
almost broken her spirit faded away to a
deep sadness.

"He's been dead four years," Carly said
softly.

"Four years?" It seemed incredible that we hadn't known. I'd googled his name more than once on the Internet, just to see if I could figure out what happened to him once he walked out of our lives so completely. Why hadn't I at least found an obituary?

"He died in Mexico," she said, as if answering the question I didn't ask. "That's why there was no record of it here."

I nodded. "I guess that makes sense. Was he ill?"

She looked over at me, her dark curls falling across her face. "He was shot to death. It was apparently a drug deal gone bad in a small border town. The local authorities kept it as quiet as possible."

"So this is what you and Elliott have been fussing about? Travis being dead?" I really couldn't see how that had turned into a source of such conflict.

She nodded her head and stared at the water bubbling in the small fountain in front of us. "It took awhile to find out for sure if the Travis that died was" — she cut her gaze to me and grimaced — "our Travis."

"And you didn't want to tell me until you knew for sure. I understand that."

She squeezed my hand. "Thanks. I knew you'd understand. I didn't see any sense in you or Mama and Daddy having to grieve if it wasn't true. Especially after you found J.D.'s body. It just brought it all so much closer and made it more real." She nodded toward the funeral home. "Just like in there. The preacher could have been preaching Travis's funeral."

I thought of his words about how quickly life passes and how awful it is to waste it. "You're right."

"The main thing Elliott and I disagree about is telling the kids."

Suddenly, the cryptic things Carly said over the last few weeks made sense. How far do you go to protect your children from pain? "You don't want to tell them."

She jerked her hand away and pushed to her feet. "I don't want to *hurt* them. I'd rather just marry Elliott and never tell them anything about their dad. At least not until they're adults."

"But Elliott feels like they should know." I stated the obvious.

"Yes! He says he doesn't want to start our lives together as a family with a deception hanging over us. Even though I understand what he means, every time I picture telling them, I just can't do it."

"So what are you going to do?"

She shrugged and stuck her hand in the cool fountain water. "I guess we're not going to do anything. We're kind of at an impasse."

My heart ached so much for her, but even Dear Pru had no wise answer for her. I stood and pulled her into a hug. "I'll be praying for you."

She nodded. "Thanks."

Dear Pru,

My husband has found someone else, and we're in the process of getting a divorce. We have a four-year-old daughter, and he wants joint custody where she will stay with me through the week and spend weekends with him. His values are very different from mine, which is one reason for the divorce. Should I agree to these conditions? If so, how can I be sure my little girl will continue to believe what I believe to be right from wrong?

Concerned Mother

Dear Mom,

You may not have a choice in the custody arrangements. Teach your child your values by living them as well as stating them. Refrain from bad-mouthing your ex, especially in front of your daughter. And pray a lot.

■ ■ ■ ■

After the funeral, I headed home and changed into my oldest T-shirt and capris. I had the rest of the day off, and I knew just what I needed. Two hours with a good book and my deck chair. Some sun, some shade, and maybe even a little nap.

I reached for my book from the shelf and recoiled as I saw the tiny flip phone. I'd stopped short of putting a blue label with DEBBIE on it, but I had put it out of the way so I'd quit getting it confused with mine. But how long was I going to keep it? I picked it up instead of the book and ran my finger over the shiny surface.

I hadn't counted on how conflicted I'd feel about Debbie's phone once I decided that Lisa definitely hadn't known about Debbie and J.D.'s "friendship." If I turned it in, they'd surely arrest Lisa, because if they had the weapon and the towel with J.D.'s blood on it, all they needed was motive. If I didn't turn it in, the guilt was going to eat me alive.

I groaned inwardly. Why hadn't I left this silver burden with Debbie that day on her porch? Sometimes I reminded myself of that obnoxious eight-year-old at every pool across America. You know, the one who feels she's responsible for everybody's well-being and can't even enjoy swimming for the weight of the responsibility. "Mama! Timmy's getting close to the deep end. Katie's not wearing her floaties. . . . Debbie threw evidence in the trash."

I started to put the phone back on the shelf then stopped. Getting rid of this once and for all would relax me more than lazing around in the backyard.

"Sorry, big guy," I murmured to Mr. Persi, who had started scampering through the house as soon as he saw me change into my yard clothes. "I'll be back in a few minutes, and we'll do it then." I glanced down at the faded jean capris and my 2004 National League Champs Cardinals shirt. I looked bad enough that I wouldn't purposely go to the store but not so bad that I'd hide in the floorboard if I had car trouble and needed help. "I won't even change clothes," I told the golden retriever. "We'll play as soon as I get back."

Neuro gave the dog a pitying look. I could imagine her saying, "Are you really buying this?"

I rubbed my hand across the cat's head. "I mean it. You could go outside, too, if you wanted to."

She jumped down, her tail high, and ran to the living room. She preferred the coolness of her window perch where she could watch us romp but still be completely pampered and comfortable.

I smiled. Who was I to question how Lisa and Larry fawned over Fluffy? I talked to my pets and filled in the blanks in their parts of the conversation.

At the thought of Lisa and her Fluffy being separated forever by jail bars, I snatched my car keys from the hook and ran out to the car.

Debbie answered the door, still wearing her black dress.

Since she had less motive than Lisa for murdering J.D., I'd decided to take my chances. "May I come in?"

She stepped back, and I walked into the tiny living room. It was neat and clean. Incredibly clean. From the way Debbie had been acting at work, I'd imagined empty wrappers and bottles lying around.

She saw my glance and apparently realized what I was thinking. "I clean when I'm upset."

I nodded. That would explain the vacuum marks still on the couch.

I shoved the phone into her hand. "I can't keep this."

She looked down at it and dropped it.

It hit the hardwood floor and flew into pieces.

Debbie gasped. "I didn't mean to do that."

We both scrambled for the pieces. "It's just the battery cover," I said. But my hands trembled as I put it back on.

"Do you think it still works?" she whispered.

"If it could survive the diner's scraps, it can surely survive this." I hit the power button, and we watched the light come on.

"Now what?" she asked.

I shrugged and set the phone on her end table. "Now it's all yours."

Panic flitted across her face. "Jenna! You can't do this. You're the one who fished it out of the trash."

"I won't make that mistake again."

Suddenly, the phone made a little beep, and we both jumped. "What was that?" I asked.

She bent down and gingerly picked it up. "I've got a missed call."

"You do?"

Her eyes widened, and she put her hand to her chest. "You don't think?" She mouthed the words, "J.D.?"

"No!" I shook my head. "Definitely not."

"What if it is? What if he's in a witness

protection program or something and he's not really dead? And I don't call him back?"

"Fine. Call him back."

She shoved the phone at me. "You do it."

"No, ma'am." I crossed my arms in front of me and conjured up a mental picture of the little eight-year-old girl at the pool. It wasn't my fault if Debbie was going off the deep end. "If you want to call, you do it."

She fumbled around and pulled up the missed-call number. "It's not his number."

Why was I not surprised?

"But it wouldn't be if he was in hiding somehow." She took a deep breath and pushed the SEND button. "It's ringing," she whispered.

I nodded, leaning toward her in spite of myself.

She obligingly stepped closer to me and held the phone where we could both hear.

"This is Chief Conner. Who is this?" an angry-sounding male voice barked.

John. Of course. Why hadn't I thought of that?

Debbie's face paled, and she raised her eyebrows at me.

"Tell him," I mouthed.

She shook her head.

"Hello?" he growled.

We just stared at each other again. "Not

my responsibility," I kept repeating to myself.

"Listen! The phone you have is evidence in a murder case. Bring it to the Lake View police station immediately. We have ways of tracing the geographical position of this phone call. It will go easier for you if you bring it here."

Debbie gasped loudly and flipped the phone shut.

She sank down on her freshly vacuumed couch and burst into tears. "This is just too much," she sobbed.

My new resolve wavered. It had been a hard day. Debbie had already been to the funeral of someone she cared about.

I sat beside her. "I'll go with you."

She reached for my hand. I took hers. She palmed the phone to me and slipped her hand away. "I can't do it, Jenna. If you do it, maybe you can calm John down."

"Ha!" Had she ever seen me with John?

She pushed her blond hair out of her face and looked at me. Tears still flowed freely down her cheeks. "I mean it. You have to at least try. I'll stay here and change clothes . . ." She ducked her head again. "And get ready to be arrested."

"Why would they arrest you?"

"Withholding evidence? Or maybe he'll

think I killed J.D. so that Lisa can't have him." She picked up a needlepoint pillow and buried her face in it.

Why had I thought I could let other people handle their own problems? I sighed. "I'll take the phone to John and talk to him."

She pulled the pillow down from her face and hugged me. "I have a confession."

"What?" I braced myself, not sure I could keep any more of her secrets.

She grabbed a tissue from the coffee table and wiped her nose. "I used to think you weren't good enough for Alex."

I blew out the breath I'd been holding. "I'm sure you were right." Debbie had never made it a secret that she would like to go out with Alex.

She sighed. "Nah, I was wrong. And if you can keep John from making a mess of this, I'll sing at your wedding."

I laughed softly. "Thanks."

"I'm Jenna Stafford. I need to see Chief Conner, please," I informed the uniformed officer at the front desk. He chewed his gum furiously for a minute while studying my face as if memorizing it for future reference. Probably thought he'd be seeing it on a wanted poster. "Please? It's important."

"Hold your horses," he said and picked

up a phone. He punched a button and spoke in a low tone, "Jenna Stafford to see you, Chief." He looked disappointed at the response but waved me toward the inner sanctum. "Go on in."

John, writing at his desk, looked up when I walked into his office. "Hey, Jenna. What can I do for you?"

I cleared my throat. I needed to get a grip on this situation quickly if I wanted it to go as I planned. I slipped into the seat across from him. "I want to make a deal with you," I began.

He held up his hand in the tradition of traffic cops everywhere and half smiled. "If you're going to tell me who you think the murderer is, I'd rather you didn't."

"No. I don't know who did it," I said quickly. "But I do have a problem connected with the murder. In a way. Only it's not, really. But you think it is."

"Instead of telling me what I think, why don't you tell me what you're talking about." John leaned back in his high-backed leather chair and crossed his arms across his chest.

I took a deep breath. "Here's the thing. The cell phone you're looking for is in my purse."

17

If you can't hunt with the big dogs,
stay on the porch.

John slapped his forehead, and red crept up his neck. "Why am I not surprised?" He held out his hand. "Where did you get it?"

I nudged my purse under my chair with one foot. "That's actually a funny story."

He wasn't laughing. "Save the story and just tell me where you got it."

"It was in the garbage, of all places."

"You know what, Jenna? Let me have the phone; then you can tell me, in little bits and pieces or however you want to, all about finding it." He snapped his fingers lightly.

"Wait. I need you to promise me something first."

This time he was the one who drew a deep breath. In fact, I thought I heard him counting under his breath. Patience is a virtue.

Maybe he was developing his. "I don't make promises, and I don't make deals. This is not television. Hand. Over. The. Phone. Now."

"Well, I did make a promise. I promised the person who had this phone that I'd talk to you about it before you made any rash decisions."

He pushed himself out of his chair and put his palms on the desk. "What I do with information received and pertinent to an ongoing investigation is not your affair. Give me the phone."

I leaned back instinctively. "The person who had this has a really good alibi for the time of the murder. I don't think she could possibly have killed J.D., but there is some information on the phone that could do her harm."

He took pity on me. Or else he was just sick of having me in his office.

"Jenna, give me a little credit. If this isn't helpful, we won't use it. And I have yet to make information public in a current investigation." His hand was still stretched toward me. "Who had the phone? Whose garbage was it in? And how did you end up with it?"

"I was gathering garbage at the diner when I spotted something. I fished around and found the phone. At first, I thought it was mine. It's exactly like mine, so that was a natural assumption." I looked at him to try and gauge his reaction.

Stone-faced.

"Anyway, when I went to check a message from Alex, there were several messages I didn't recognize. Then I found my phone in my purse."

"So who does the phone belong to?" He held out his hand. "Never mind. Just let me have the phone, and I'll find out."

"I'd like to." I glanced at his unyielding face. "The thing is, the person who had this phone doesn't want Lisa to know that she had it."

"This phone is evidence in a murder investigation. So far I've purposely avoided asking you how long ago you found it. But you don't even want to know what it would be like if you're charged with withholding evidence or being an accessory to murder." John glared at me. "Tell me what you know and quit playing games."

"Okay." I caved. "J.D. and Debbie were just starting to see each other behind Lisa's back. Debbie doesn't want Lisa to find out." I reached down and picked up my purse. "They were planning to tell Lisa, but then he got killed."

"Or J.D. went ahead and told Lisa, and she got mad and shot him," John murmured. He looked quickly at me. "Ignore that. I was just thinking aloud."

I didn't like the direction his thoughts were going. "I thought Lisa had an alibi." I pulled the phone out of my purse and laid it on the desk.

"Not an airtight one." He looked me in the eye. "But you're sure Debbie does?" He picked up the phone and flipped it open as if the murderer's name was written in the keys.

"Well, she was washing dishes in the kitchen at the diner." But did she have an airtight alibi? I couldn't say positively that she hadn't left the diner for a few minutes. How long would it take to run out back, shoot an unsuspecting victim, and dash back inside? And even follow me out and knock me in the head? Anyone at the diner easily could have done it. But there was the fact that she was possibly the only one who knew he was supposed to be out there. Unless he had a whole bevy of secret girlfriends.

"So you can say for sure that she never went outside?" John searched my face as if he could see the questions running through my mind.

I reluctantly shook my head. "Not positively."

"Well, then, don't expect me to make you any promises. I will do what is necessary to bring a killer to justice. But I will not harm any innocent bystanders if I can help it."

It wasn't the promise I wanted, but I had to be content with that.

"Reporting for duty," I said as I breezed into the kitchen. Getting rid of Debbie's phone yesterday had done a lot to lighten my burden of responsibility. If I could keep Lisa out of jail and figure out how to solve Carly's problems, I'd be batting a thousand.

Carly smiled at me. "Just in time." She wiped her hands on her apron as she went to the large refrigerator for more ingredients. Whatever she was cooking, the aroma was delicious. Alice nodded to me from the stove. Funny how well they were working together now when Alice and Harvey had only about a week left on their agreement to help out.

"You should bottle that smell," I told them as I got my own apron and checked the pocket. Yes, my order pad and pencil were there. I was ready for business.

Carly grinned. "If only we could figure out how."

271

I was glad to see her smiling. She'd told me last night on the phone that the funeral had been therapeutic for her in a way. And that with God's help she was closer to figuring things out. I'd been praying ever since that God would work it out. He was so much better at handling things than I was.

"Anything I need to know before I go out there?" I asked.

She shrugged. "Harvey's seating folks, and Susan and Vini have their hands full. Debbie called and said she's under the weather." She sent me a questioning look, and I shrugged. I'd told Carly the whole thing on the phone last night. And I didn't know anything new.

I pushed the swinging door and was immersed in the hubbub made by happy diners. I waved to Harvey to let him know my section of tables could be put into use and headed to the menu stand. The next couple of hours passed in a blur. I had the fleeting reflection that this job wasn't so bad. Hard, but interesting. Mostly hard, though. My thoughts were scattered when a familiar voice trumpeted my name.

I looked up.

"Hey, Miss Lady, how much longer are you chained to that apron?" Jolene wended her way through a maze of tables to me, conversing the entire way. Presumably with me, but loudly enough for it to be a community conversation. "I came to tell you bye-bye."

"Have a seat, Jolene," I murmured, in the hopes she would follow my example and talk more quietly. "Let me bring you a glass of tea."

I left a menu on the table and went to the counter. I returned with her tea. "Can I get you anything to eat?"

"Nah, sweetie. Thanks, but I ate a late breakfast at the hotel. I just thought you and me might have a little heart-to-heart before I head out."

"I can't leave, but I can take a break for a few minutes. Let me clear it with Harvey." I went to his station and explained that I would be on break for the next ten minutes, grabbed myself a glass of tea, and went back to sit with Jolene.

"So, you're heading out, huh? Where to?"

"You know, girl, I been thinking about that a lot. I ain't had what you might call roots since I was a little kid in pigtails. Now I got this money, compliments of Jimmy-boy, God rest his soul, and I think I might just make a down payment on a little house somewheres. My granny's place in Texas comes to mind. I 'magine her old house is tore down, but I b'lieve I could find me something reasonable around there. I might just go back to waitressing my own self. I'd make enough to pay the bills, and I'd have a life like most folks have." She beamed at me like a first grader showing her mother a good report card.

"Jolene, I think that's a great idea."

"Seems kinda funny, don't it? Jimmy and me never did have what most folks would think of as a good marriage. He never was one to make a honest living. More times than not, I was the one who took care of him." She shook her head in wonder. "But here I am, fixin' to buy a house, and it's thanks to him. The Lord surely does work in mysterious ways, don't He?"

"He sure does," I agreed. I took a sip of tea. "Jolene, I hope things work out well for you."

"Why, I'm sure they will, chickie. You can't keep a good woman down. Speaking of women, you never did introduce me to Jimmy's latest flame."

I sent a brief prayer of thanksgiving that neither Debbie nor Lisa was at the diner.

"No, I didn't. And she's not here right now."

"Ah, well, I guess I'll live without meeting her. I'm ready to blow this burg and hit that little watering hole in the next county. Then I'm off to Texas." She stood and leaned down to envelop me in a scented, smothering hug. "Don't take life too serious, girlfriend. It'll be over before you know it." She gave me a cheery grin and headed to the door. She detoured through Vini's section and pinched his cheek before he could dodge. "Been a pleasure seeing you, sweet cakes. Every single time." And Jolene Highwater was gone. The effect was of a gentle breeze after a howling windstorm.

The ringing of my cell phone jerked me to attention.

"Hello?"

"Jenna?" Debbie's voice could've scorched my ear. "Forget about me singing at your wedding." She spat the words at me.

"Why?" I replied guardedly. But she talked right over me.

"I've spent the last hour at the police station. Doesn't that sound like fun? Well, it's not. Being accused of murder is not a joke at all. I knew this would happen. But nooo. You had to take it into your own hands. Well, from now on, just butt out of my life."

I bit back the reminder that she'd asked me to take the phone to John and talk to him on her behalf. And that I'd done exactly that. "Debbie, calm down. Did John actually accuse you of murder? That doesn't sound right."

"John didn't come right out and accuse me of murder." She was a little less agitated but still touchy. "But I could tell he was suspicious. He really gave me the third degree."

"Well, he would have to question you. After all," I pointed out in a reasonable tone, "you withheld a valuable piece of evidence." She began sputtering, but I continued, "He isn't still suspicious of you, is he? I mean, he didn't threaten to lock you up or warn you not to leave town, did he?"

"No," she said quietly, as if my words were finally soaking in. "And he did say he wouldn't tell Lisa unless he has to. So that's a plus."

"See? Doing the right thing is good." I reminded myself of Pollyanna.

A muted growl from the other end of the phone warned me to tread lightly. "And think of it this way: You won't have to worry about it anymore."

"That's true." She was almost back to normal. "Tell Carly I'll be in for the evening shift." She hung up without saying goodbye, but I was thankful to get through that conversation with a whole ear. I went to the kitchen to give Carly an update. We had the break room to ourselves, so I told her all about Debbie's irate phone call.

"Well, it's best for Debbie to get it out in the open. I'm sorry if she hurt your feelings" — she smiled at me — "but you were right. And getting your ears blistered is a small price to see that the right thing is done."

I turned off the water. Was that my phone ringing? I hoped it wasn't an emergency, because whoever it was would have to wait until I dried, dressed, and towel-dried my hair.

Finally, wrapped in my robe, I checked my voice messages. "Miss Stafford, this is Lawrence Hall." It took me a second to realize it was Larry. That cleared up the mystery of which name he went by. "Bob Pryor asked me to call you and tell you that Lisa's been taken into custody." He left his number in case I needed more information then ended the message.

I glanced at the clock hanging by the front door. It was only 8:30. I considered my options. Dry my hair and go on to bed. Toss and turn all night wondering what happened to Lisa. Or go down to the police station and offer moral support and comfort to Bob and Wilma. Not to mention have a little talk with John.

An easy decision.

I quickly dressed, combed out my hair, and stuck it up in a messy bun. At a quarter till nine, I pulled in front of the station and headed in.

"I'd like to see the chief, please," I said to the desk sergeant.

"I'm sorry, ma'am; he's in a meeting at the moment."

"Will you tell him that Jenna Stafford is waiting out here to see him?" I smiled at him. "I just need to talk to him for a minute."

"I'm sorry, ma'am." He leaned toward me. "He told me not to interrupt him."

"Well, I'll just sit out here and wait if you don't mind." I turned to sit in one of the chairs near the desk.

"If you'd like, there's a waiting area just down the hall on your left." He pointed. "There are some people in there already, but the chairs are a little more comfortable."

"Thanks. I'll go down there. Will you be sure Chief Conner gets my message?"

"Yes, ma'am. I'll tell him as soon as he comes out."

Bob and Wilma were huddled together in the corner when I walked in. They wore identical shell-shocked expressions.

Bob stood and came toward me. "Jenna, thanks so much for coming. We've hired an attorney, but he has to drive in from Little Rock."

I gave him a one-armed hug. "I'm so sorry."

He returned my hug, but as soon as he released me, he began pacing. "He said for Lisa not to answer any questions, but I don't know what she's saying in there. They wouldn't let us go in with her."

"I'm sure her lawyer will be in soon." I bent down and gave Wilma a hug. "He'll get this straightened out." I sat down next to her.

"Bob, stop pacing." Wilma leaned her head back and closed her eyes.

"Jenna, you've been around this kind of thing. Can you think of anything else we can do?" Bob sat back down in the chair on the other side of Wilma.

"You just need to stay strong." I wished I had a better answer for them.

"You know, you spend your life protecting your child, and then something out of the blue like this happens." Tears rolled from Wilma's closed eyes and made tracks down her cheeks. "It makes you wonder. . . ." Her voice trailed off. I held my breath while I waited for her to say something more. Or for Bob to answer her.

When no one said anything, I patted Wilma on the back. "Why don't I go and get us something to drink from the vending machine?" I left them to their painful memories and headed out the door. "I'll be right back."

I walked down the hall to the outer office where I had seen the vending machines. A uniformed sleeve brushed my arm, and I looked up into Seth's smiling eyes.

"Hey, Nancy Drew. What are you doing here?"

"Larry called me." I stuck some bills into the machine and hit the button for water.

"Lisa is in there with John right now. I feel sorry for her folks, but we've got enough on that girl to put her away for life now that we have the motive."

18

What goes around, comes around.

I stared at Seth. Now they had a motive. Which I had handed to them on a silver platter. Lisa was frighteningly self-centered, and if she had known her boyfriend and her best friend were cheating on her, well, murder wasn't so far-fetched. But I was convinced she had no idea. I just had to convince John.

"I don't think she did it, Seth." I hit the button again and watched another bottle fall out.

His eyebrows drew together. "She had motive, the weapon belonged to her and had her fingerprints on it, his blood was on a towel found in her car, and her alibi won't hold water." He ticked each item off on his fingers. "And now she's lawyering up. You just don't want to believe it because of her parents."

"I don't want to believe it because she didn't do it, Seth. Is there any way I can talk to John?" I clutched the three bottles of water to my chest.

"As soon as her lawyer gets here, he'll probably want to talk to her alone. When he does, John will come out." He'd no sooner said that than the front door burst open and a distinguished-looking, black-haired man in a three-piece suit pushed open the double glass doors and rushed up to the desk. "And I think he just arrived." Seth said the last words in a whisper.

After the desk sergeant showed the attorney to the room where Lisa waited, I dropped off the water to Bob and Wilma then hurried back into the hallway so I could catch John as he came out of the interrogation room.

I touched his arm when he stepped out the door. "John, could I have a minute?"

"You again? You're just like a bad penny." It didn't sound like a joke when he said it. "You have exactly" — he looked at his watch — "five minutes. That's it." He motioned me into his office. "And I'm only giving you that because you came through with the motive."

"This is all wrong. Lisa didn't kill J.D." I pushed the door shut. "She had no idea he was cheating on her. So she had no motive."

"Jenna, just go on home and let me do my job." Déjà vu all over again. Hadn't he said those exact words when he brought my nephew, Zac, in for questioning in an earlier murder case? And look how wrong he'd been then.

"I'm not trying to keep you from doing your job. I'm just trying to keep you from looking like a fool." I resisted the urge to stomp my foot for emphasis. "I'm telling you, she had no reason to kill him. I've talked to her about it."

"Riiight." He drew out the word and shook his head. "And you think she'd just confess to you if she did it?" He looked at his watch. "I guess Bob has convinced you that she's being framed?"

"I believe she is being framed. If she'd used her gun, she'd have taken it back home with her and gotten rid of it. And why would she put a bloody towel under her seat?"

He flinched.

"Everybody knows about that. I heard it at the diner."

He nodded. "Small towns."

"And like I said, she didn't know about Debbie and J.D., so you don't have motive."

He tapped his watch as if maybe it had

stopped. "Look, I feel sorry for her parents just like you do, but I can't let a murderer go free because I feel sorry for her family."

"You're making a mistake if you charge her with murder."

"And you're making a mistake if you continue to try to tell me how to do my job." His voice rose. "But, for your information, I haven't officially charged her. Yet." Another glance at his watch. "Your time is up."

Bob and Wilma were still sitting exactly as they had been when I first walked in. The only difference was the unopened bottle of water each held.

I sank into the empty chair beside Wilma and put my arm around her but could find no comforting words. The two of them were silent as the grave. I cleared my throat. "Did Lisa give them her alibi?" I hated to pry, but both John and Seth had mentioned that it wouldn't hold up.

"Yes." Bob closed his mouth on that one word. Okay, this was weird. He had been so forthcoming before. Now suddenly he clammed up?

"And the police didn't believe her?" I was fishing for information.

"They believed her. They just said she had time to drive by and shoot J.D. first." He looked down at the floor. "Thanks so much for coming by, Jenna. Lisa's lawyer is here now, and I guess there's nothing you can do." He looked at Wilma. "Except take Wilma home for me."

She shook her head. "I'm staying with you."

"No, honey, go on home. You'll need to get some rest so you can help us tomorrow." He gently took her hand and helped her to her feet. "Please go home. I don't want to have to worry about both my girls."

Still clutching her water, Wilma kissed him on the cheek. "Okay. But call me if you know anything. No matter what time it is."

After I walked Wilma in and was pulling out of her drive way, my phone rang. I flipped it open. "Hello?"

"Jen?" Carly's voice trembled.

"What's wrong?"

She laughed. "Nothing."

"Nothing? You sound like you've been crying."

"Happy tears this time."

"Oh?" I slapped the steering wheel with one hand. "Spill it, Sister."

"Elliott asked me to marry him. And I said yes!"

"Carly, that's fantastic." I forced myself

not to ask any questions about the Travis situation. If they'd worked it out, that's what mattered.

"Jenna, he took me out to eat, and after dessert he got down on one knee." She laughed again. "You should see the ring. It's perfect!"

Tears pricked at my eyes. "I can't wait to see it."

"Then he told me that if I chose not to tell the kids about Travis, he would respect that, because he wasn't going to throw away our happiness by being stubborn."

"I knew my future brother-in-law was a great guy."

"He's a wise man, too," she said softly. "I've been praying hard about it, and I've decided to tell them. And Mama and Daddy."

"Oh, Carly . . ." Relief coursed through me. "I'm proud of you."

"Thanks, but I want more than your admiration. I want your support."

I turned my signal on and negotiated the turn into my driveway. "Name the time and place. I don't have to go into the gym until three tomorrow. And if I need to, I can get someone to cover for me."

"Tomorrow morning for breakfast."

I killed the motor. "At the diner?" Strange

place for a family meeting.

She laughed. "Since Alice and Harvey only have a couple more days, I'm letting them handle the Saturday morning crowd alone. I'm cooking at my place."

"You sure you don't want me to pick up some bacon biscuits?"

"Cooking will help me stay calm. Just come hungry."

The next morning when I got to Carly's cabin, she met me at the kitchen door.

"Calm yet?" I murmured as I wiped flour from her face.

She wrinkled her nose at me. "I'm glad you're here. I can't decide whether to tell them about the engagement after I tell them the other or not."

"Why don't you just play it by ear? Is Elliott coming?"

She shook her head. "He thought the kids — especially Zac — would be able to show their true feelings better if he wasn't here."

"He's probably right." Zac had been ten when his dad left, and even though he seemed to be crazy about Elliott, he'd need time to grieve.

"The twins will be —"

A knock on the door sounded in the middle of Carly's sentence.

"— fine," she said as she went to let Mama and Daddy in.

Mama held out a glass bottle of orange juice. "Fresh squeezed," she said and hugged Carly.

"She squeezed it herself," Daddy assured us.

I stared from Mama to Carly. "Why didn't I get any of those genes?"

"No one wants a carbon copy of themselves, dear," Mama said. "You're unique." She started pulling glasses from the cabinet for the orange juice. "Speaking of which, are y'all going to Tiffany's shower this afternoon?"

"Yes," I said. "We both are." Carly had protested, but I'd insisted.

"Want me to pick you up?" Carly asked her.

"Sure."

"Jenna?"

"I need to go on to the club to work after the shower, so I'll take my own car."

The twins came bounding in. "Is breakfast ready?"

Carly nodded. "Go get your brother and go to the table."

Forty-five minutes later, we'd all finished our bacon, sausage, eggs, and homemade biscuits. Zac pushed back from the table.

"I've got to go, Mom. I'm supposed to meet the guys at the basketball court."

Carly held up her hand and laid her napkin down. "Not yet. Let's all go in the living room." She stood.

Zac frowned. "Why?"

"Just because," she said softly.

"Don't you want us to clean off the table first?" Rachel asked.

"No," Carly said. "We'll do it later."

"Uh-oh," I heard Hayley whisper as we made our way into the other room. "It must be something bad."

In the living room, the twins sank to the floor with their backs against the paneled wall. Zac slumped spinelessly in an over-stuffed chair. I sat beside Mama and Daddy on the sofa.

Carly stood in front of the blank TV and faced us. She gave a nervous half laugh. "I know now why people start off by saying, 'There's no easy way to say this.' Because there's really not."

Daddy put his arm around Mama and gave Carly a gentle smile. "Honey, bad news usually goes better quickly. If it's good, then you can drag it out."

She stared at him as if absorbing his words. "Okay then." She looked at the kids. "It's about your dad, Travis."

The twins looked mildly curious, but Zac snapped to attention. I heard an indrawn breath from Mama. Daddy tightened his arm around her shoulders.

"What about him?" Zac's voice was as brittle as ice, his face expressionless.

Carly looked one more time at Daddy as if weighing his advice, then looked back at Zac. "He's dead, honey."

Zac's stern demeanor melted. His eyes widened, and he looked like he was going to be sick. "When did he die?"

"Four years ago."

Zac recoiled, and I could see him doing the math, calculating where he was and how old he'd been when his dad died. "How?"

Carly hesitated, and I could tell by the rapid blinking that she was fighting tears.

"We have a right to know," Zac said harshly.

I glanced at the twins. They were quiet, but their expressions were more curious than upset.

Carly's brows drew together. "You don't have to demand information, Zac. I'll tell you everything I know."

"That'll be a switch," he muttered.

"Zac. I just found this out."

"They didn't notify you when he died?" he said in a disbelieving tone.

Carly shook her head. "I hired a private investigator a few weeks ago to try to find him. And this is what he found out." Her voice quivered.

Zac pulled a pillow off the floor and clutched it to his chest. "So how did he die?"

"He was shot in a little border town in Mexico," Carly said.

I could see Zac's brain working. He really is an intelligent young man. A variety of emotions flitted across his face.

"Shot? Was he into drugs? Or something else illegal?" His voice was thin.

"Honey, we don't know what happened. Just that he was found in a seedy part of town and had been seen with a known dealer. I'm sorry."

Zac shrugged. "Does Elliott know?"

Carly shot me a look of panic.

"Why?" I asked.

Zac's mouth was a straight, tight line. Finally, he spoke. "I just figured if he found out that was the kind of dad we had, he might not want anything to do with us."

Carly put her hand to her mouth. The tears she'd been fighting filled her eyes. "Zac, Elliott loves you."

"And us," Rachel said firmly.

"And you girls, too," Carly agreed. "And he knows that no one is all good or all bad."

"Remember that story I used to tell y'all?" Daddy spoke up. "How there are two wolves inside of you all the time fighting to win?"

The twins nodded quickly. Zac hesitated, but he nodded, too.

"A good wolf and a bad wolf," Hayley said.

"And which one is going to win?" Daddy asked softly.

"The one you feed," Zac muttered.

"Your daddy fed the wrong one, honey," Mama said. "But that has nothing to do with who you are."

Carly gave me a questioning look, and I nodded. We could all use some good news.

"I have one more thing to tell you all," Carly said.

"More about Da — him?" Zac asked.

She shook her head. "This is about us. All of us." She smiled at her kids. "Elliott and I are getting married."

"Married?" Rachel said, her voice high. "Whoo-hoo!" She jumped up and tackled her mama. Her sister was right behind her. They danced around Carly. Mama and Daddy stood and each reached over the top of the twins to hug her. When they stepped back, Carly looked at Zac. "It's a lot to take in all at once," she said. I knew she was giving him a chance to retreat quietly.

He stood and nodded. "It is. But it'll be cool not to be the only guy around this house." A hint of a smile touched his solemn expression. "Maybe I won't be so outnumbered anymore."

And just like that, he was gone to play basketball, the twins hot on his heels. Carly smiled at Mama and me. "Who wants to see my ring?"

"Now I'm the one who's outnumbered," Daddy said, but he did stay to admire his daughter's engagement ring.

The only comfort I had was that Mama looked as disconcerted as I felt. She gave me a weak smile and placed the paper plate on her head. I did the same.

Carly giggled. "I wish I had a camera."

"Hush and put your own plate on," I growled.

"Now use these markers, and without taking the plate off your head, draw your idea of Tiffany's dream house. When we're done, she'll choose her favorite drawing, and the winner will get a prize." The tanned blond beamed at us as if she were giving us all a wonderful opportunity.

"The prize had better be a house in Florida," I muttered to Carly.

"Right on the beach," she agreed.

Tiffany, sitting next to me, snickered. "Y'all do look ridiculous."

"I think the bride should have to play, too," Denise said loudly from the other side of Tiffany. "And I don't think John would want me reaching up. Didn't they used to say that wasn't good for the baby?"

"That's an old wives' tale," one of the Anderson sisters said from across the circle, clutching her paper plate on her head.

"Look it up on the Internet," said the other sister, who was eighty if she was a day. "You'll see." She turned to the hostess. "Are you going to tell us when to draw?"

"Be patient. Everyone has to have her plate on her head before I can start," the blond said with a pointed look at Amelia.

The mother of the bride lifted her tanned arm and placed the paper plate on her head.

While Tiffany was selecting the winner, I wandered over to the table to refill my empty punch cup. I picked out some almonds and cashews and put them on my small crystal plate. One of the Anderson sisters — I could never tell them apart — strolled up beside me. "Don't you work over at that health club for Bob Pryor?"

"Yes, ma'am." I added a few mints to my plate.

"That poor man. I heard that he may lose

everything, even his house." She ladled some punch into her own cup and gave me a sideways look. "Is that true?"

"I haven't heard that." I set my cup down on the table and nibbled on an almond. "Why would he?"

"That hoity-toity daughter of his." She sipped her red punch. "She's in all kinds of trouble."

"Oh." *Now* I knew what she meant. "You mean because the police think she might have had something to do with murdering J.D. Finley?"

"That good for nothing Finley boy? His grandma spent her life's savings bailing him out of one thing after another." She wiped her lips daintily with her napkin. "But that's not what I meant," she said impatiently. "I was talking about the gambling."

"Gambling?" I parroted. "I don't know what you mean." I glanced around the room to see if anyone was listening to our conversation. Everyone was enthralled with the dream house pictures. "Bob hasn't mentioned anything about gambling."

"That girl of his. She's lost a lot of money over there at that gambling place in Mississippi." She tipped up her punch cup and downed the remains. "Tunica. That's where she said she was when that boy was shot."

She wiped her lips. "And from what I hear, she goes there all the time. Musta cost her daddy a pretty penny."

"Come on everyone, sit back down," the blond hostess called. "We're going to play another game."

"Tiffany, you leave the room," she said. "Just go out in the hall and wait awhile." She made shooing motions with her hands. "We'll call you back in a few minutes."

Miss Anderson and I walked back to find seats. Amelia scooted over to sit beside me.

As soon as Tiffany left, we were given a piece of paper and a pencil with instructions to write as many facts as we could about her. What she was wearing, her birth date, her fiancé's name, her wedding date — the list was long. I held my blank paper in my hand and tried to remember exactly what color Tiffany was wearing.

"Psst." Amelia jogged my arm. "Just forget it."

"Forget what she was wearing? I thought we were trying to remember." I tapped my pencil against my teeth then threw a guilty look at Mama. She always hated when I did that.

"Forget about finding out about Ricky," she whispered as she wrote a couple of things on her paper. "I've decided we don't need to know." I sneaked a peek over her shoulder. Oh yeah. Yellow sweater. I remembered now. Blue skirt. Surprising that Amelia had paid so much attention.

"She's going to marry him anyway," she said out of the side of her mouth. "So I'm butting out." She wrote several more items down. I resisted the urge to copy them onto my sheet.

"Okay. If you're sure." I'd exhausted all my resources anyway. Seth and John.

I quickly wrote Ricky Richards down on my paper. At least I had one answer.

After Tiffany was called back into the room and we went over the answers, I realized that all the guests, even Carly, had listed more information than I had. And Amelia, who got every answer correct, was the lucky winner of the bow-covered paper plate hat.

As I helped carry things to the car with Marge, Tiffany, and Amelia, Marge congratulated Amelia on having the most correct answers. "Well, she is my daughter," Amelia said dryly. "I probably know her better than most people." She glanced at Tiffany as she put a pile of gifts in the trunk of the Prius. "I'm aware of those little tricks she thinks she is pulling on me."

Tiffany turned to stare at her. "What tricks?"

Amelia continued to address Marge and me. "Dressing frumpy and wearing no makeup. But I've seen pictures of her dressed to the nines and beautiful."

Tiffany reddened. "I don't know what you're talking about, Mother."

"Of course you do, darling," Amelia drawled. "I even understand why you do it."

"Really?" Tiffany widened her eyes. "Why don't you explain it then?"

"You resent the fact that I sent you away to boarding school." Amelia glanced at Marge. "And that I nag you all the time about your clothes, your weight, everything." She smiled. "That about sum it up?"

I could see the emotions flit across Tiffany's face. Surprise, anger, sadness, and finally resignation. "Yeah, I guess it does."

"Someday after you have children, I'll explain it all to you. Although by that time you may understand." She looked at Tiffany. "No, you're stronger than I ever was. You won't ever get it."

Marge looked at her sister and niece then at my face, which I could tell was red. "It's nice to see you two finally clearing the air, but maybe we should continue this at home?"

That idea definitely had my vote.

Midafternoon, I'd just gotten to the athletic club when Bob walked in, still in his rumpled clothes from the night before. "Jenna? I need to see you in the office."

I dropped the stack of towels I was putting away and hurried to the office on his heels.

"I have something I want to ask you." He shut the door.

"Is it Lisa?" I blurted out.

"Is what Lisa? Where?" Bob cast a confused look around the office as if he expected his jailed daughter to pop up from behind the file cabinet or crawl from under the ratty rug.

"What did you want to ask me?"

"Oh. Have a seat." Uh-oh. This wasn't sounding too good.

I sank into a chair in front of the desk.

He cleared his throat. "I've decided to sell you the club."

19

Could've talked all day and not said that.

"If you want it, I'll start the paperwork immediately. We agreed on a price three years ago, and I'll honor that. I know I promised to finance, but I'm in a bind, so you'll have to find your own financing."

My heart pounded. Now that I knew about Lisa's gambling problem, everything made sense. Even though I'd been waiting forever for Bob to actually come through with the sale, it bothered me that he was doing it under duress.

He continued, "Any bank in town knows the Lake View Athletic Club is a solid business, so you shouldn't have any trouble getting backing. The books are in order, and I'll send them to whatever bank or S & L you want me to."

I just sat there. I didn't know what to say. My turn for throat clearing. "I appreciate the offer," I finally choked out. "But I need to think it over. Can I get back to you on it?"

"I need a decision by tonight. This is a one-time chance, Jenna. I've got other potential buyers, but I promised you first shot, so I'm giving it to you."

My eyes widened. He was going to sell the business. And quickly. To me or to someone else. "Can't I have until Monday?"

He shook his head. "I have to know by tonight."

"In that case, I'll need the rest of the afternoon off."

He nodded. "I understand."

I stood, grabbed my purse from the filing cabinet drawer, and walked out to my car. My mind whirled as I drove away.

When I got to the edge of town, I pulled my cell phone out and punched in Alex's number. He had gotten home during the shower this afternoon. Straight to voice mail. I left a message and pulled into the Stafford Cabins' drive like a homing pigeon.

For a while, I walked the banks of the lake, mindlessly skipping stones until my phone rang.

"Hi, honey, I got your message."

My heart warmed just hearing his voice. I still hadn't fully realized the fact that I didn't have to make big decisions alone anymore. "Welcome home. I'm sorry, I know you're tired from your trip, but are you free for a few minutes?"

"I'm always free for you. What do you need?"

"An ear. You got one?"

"Hey, you're in luck! I've got two. Where are you?"

I told him, and ten minutes later he was there, pulling me into his arms and kissing me soundly. "Oh, wait," he said as he released me. "It was my ears you wanted. I got confused."

I laughed, amazed by how much lighter my heart was already. Whatever we decided together, God would work it out.

He took my hand, and we walked along the lakeshore. He glanced over at me. "So what's on your mind?"

I frowned. "Bob wants to sell me the club."

"So how come you're acting like he sold it out from under you?"

I tugged him to a stop. "Well, for one thing, he's not financing it, which was part of the promise. For another, I have to let him know tonight. And he threatened me. Sort of. He mentioned that he has other people interested in buying."

"So what do you think is going on?"

"I think Lisa's been arrested and has a gambling problem, and he needs money."

He turned me to face him. "And why does that make this decision difficult?"

"I don't know. I feel guilty, I guess, like a vulture circling its prey." Even though no one was in sight, I instinctively lowered my voice. "I *am* the one who turned in the cell phone that gave John the motive to arrest her."

He brushed my hair back with his free hand. "Did you do that to hurt Lisa? Or because it was the right thing to do?"

"Because it was the right thing to do."

"So that has nothing to do with this. From the way I understand what you're telling me, Bob is going to sell the club. With or without you. Right?"

I nodded.

"Let me ask you something. If Bob had made this offer before you knew about Lisa's problem and before she got arrested, what would you have done?"

"Jumped on it with both feet."

"Well, then, get on your jumping shoes, water girl. If it was a good deal then, it's a good deal now."

"What about all the paperwork?"

He dropped a kiss on my forehead. "Lucky for you, you're looking at the king of paperwork. Let's go find a banker who wants to get rid of some money."

"At this hour on a Saturday?"

He grinned. "I'm also the king of connections."

"Who knew I was marrying royalty?" I held up one finger. "Just a sec." I palmed my phone, flipped it open, and punched in a phone number. "Hello, Bob? It's Jenna. I've made my decision. Start the paperwork, and I'll start the financing process."

When I hung up, I looked at Alex. "I can't believe it's really happening." I grinned.

He put his arms around me. "You're not going to get so busy with your new business that you'll want to postpone our wedding, are you?"

I smirked. "And give up my chance to be your queen? Never."

Monday morning Bob and I signed the initial paperwork.

"We'll keep this under our hats until it's all finished," he said.

I nodded. "As far as everyone is concerned, I'll just start back to work for you full-time today."

"Doesn't your sister need some notice?"

I laughed. "She practically pushed me out the door. She knows where my heart is."

"That's one reason I'm so glad you're the one buying it," Bob said softly.

"Thanks. The bank says they'll have the financing by Friday. I'll take that day off to take care of everything. We'll sign the paperwork in Alex's office that afternoon."

"And you can celebrate Friday night as the new owner," Bob finished.

I laughed. "Yeah, probably by just coming here and soaking in the fact that it's mine."

Later that afternoon, Bob paged me to the office.

He looked up from his desk when I came in, his eyes wild. "Jenna," he said, his voice hoarse. "Gail can run the club awhile. I need you to drive me somewhere."

I took in the fine sheen of sweat on his brow and his pale complexion.

"Bob?" The words "heart attack" flashed across my mind like a neon sign. "Are you okay? Should I call an ambulance?"

"Ambulance? What are you talking about? Can't you drive me downtown without making a federal case of it?" He gave me an irritated glance. Okay. Something was seriously wrong. Bob could be exasperating at times, but I'd never seen him like this. I grabbed my keys and followed him out to the parking lot. As I slid behind the wheel, I glanced at him. He looked more normal, but his hand shook as he fastened his seat belt.

I put the car in gear and headed out of the parking lot. "Look, Bob, if something's wrong, it might help if you tell me about it."

"If something's wrong? My only child is in jail and likely to go through a nasty murder trial. She's taking the rap for some-one else." He cleared his throat. "I'm going to fix that. Take me to the police depart-ment." And he clamped his lips shut.

I glanced at him, wondering if he had a weapon hidden somewhere. Was he going to bust Lisa out of jail? When we arrived at the station, I pulled up to let him out, but he motioned sharply to the small parking lot next to the department, and I obediently pulled in.

"Come on. Let's go in," he said gruffly.

I frowned. What did he think I was going to do? Play Bonnie to his Clyde?

He glanced back at me. "I may need you to back me up. I'm not sure how this is go-ing to go," he muttered.

I trailed him into the building.

"I need to see Chief Conner immediately," he barked to the young guy behind the desk. We were ushered into John's office where John courteously offered us chairs.

I sank into the ugly plastic chair, but Bob remained standing. He leaned over John's desk, placing both hands flat on the surface.

"John. I'm here to confess."

"What did you do, Bob? Let your business license expire?"

"I'm serious. I killed that guy."

I was glad I was sitting down. John glanced my way with raised eyebrows. I held my arms out, palms up. I was just the driver.

"Bob," John said sternly, "what you're doing is a serious offense. You can't present false information to a police officer. Why don't you go on home and think this over some more?"

"What you're doing is illegal, too. I confessed to a serious crime. You have to question me."

"Fine. What were you doing the night of the crime?" John spoke in an official tone.

"Drat it, John. I'm serious." Bob glared at him. "I killed a man. I'm confessing to it. You have no choice but to lock me up."

"Bob, go on home. Your daughter is fine." John patted him on the shoulder. "Things will look better in the morning."

Bob's sudden lunge was so unexpected that John had no time to react. I leaped to my feet. Two officers rushed into the room in response to the shouts, or maybe to the noise the chair and desk made when Bob turned them over. They cuffed Bob a little roughly, but their chief was nursing a bruised eye, so I couldn't blame them.

"Jenna . . ." Bob turned his head as they shoved him out of the room. "Go by and tell Wilma what happened."

Thanks a lot, boss.

Wilma didn't take it any better than I thought she would.

"This is so crazy. First my child; now my husband. What is John thinking? Bob could no more kill someone on purpose than I could."

"Um, Wilma, to be fair, Bob didn't give him much choice. He sort of slugged John."

"Oh my goodness. This is making Bob so crazy. He's never hit anyone in his life. He was all about the 'peace and love' thing. What was he thinking?" She twisted the towel in her hands. "I have to do something. Let me see. What do I need to do?"

"Why don't you lie down?" I suggested. "I'll get you a cold glass of water."

"Lie down?" She stared at me as if I'd suggested she leap off a cliff. "Why would I lie down? And I'm not thirsty, thanks. I need a plan." She twisted the towel harder then stretched it out. She looked up at me as if she'd forgotten I was there. "Jenna, run along, honey. I've got things to do."

This family was in serious need of therapy. I left before I needed it, too, and headed back to the gym, where I spent the rest of my shift fielding questions about Bob from Gail and Dave.

"This better be good," I muttered. I hated being awakened by a ringing phone. My heart was in high gear and my brain wasn't engaged. Never a good scenario.

"Hello?"

"Jenna?" A voice I didn't recognize. I struggled to see caller ID, but my eyes were blurry from sleep. "I need your help."

"Who is this?"

"Oh, sorry. This is John. Could you come to the station, please? I can send a car for you if you wish."

"I have a car, thanks." This was a strange conversation, but I tried to be polite.

"Did I wake you up?" John's voice was tinged with amusement.

"What time is it?"

"Um, about six o'clock." He sounded a little sheepish.

"Then you woke me up."

"Sorry. I didn't look at the clock until just now." But Wilma's dwon here and she's asking for you."

"I'll be there in thirty minutes." I rolled out of bed and headed to the bathroom.

I was only a couple of minutes late, and I knew I looked like a contestant for the police lineup. I was ushered straight to John's office where Wilma occupied the chair I'd sat in yesterday. Compared to how she looked, I was ready for a beauty contest. Her hair stood out every which way, and her eyes were swollen and bloodshot. Almost as bad as John's eye, I noticed.

And she was crying. Not loud wails, just a soft, hopeless weeping. I took the chair next to her and put an arm around her shoulder.

"Wilma?" My mind went blank. What do you say to a woman whose husband and daughter are both in jail?

"She came to confess," John spoke wryly. "Tell us one more time what happened, Mrs. Pryor."

"I was mad at J.D. for breaking up Lisa's marriage. I followed him to the diner and shot him with Lisa's gun." She spoke in a monotone, and her voice was so low I had to strain to hear it.

"Will you sit with her just a minute, Jenna?" John left the room but returned shortly leading Bob. When Bob realized Wilma was in the office, he stepped forward and took her hands.

"Honey, what are you doing down here? Didn't you read the note I left?"

"Note? No. I didn't find a note." She glanced at me and back to him again. "Jenna stopped by and told me where you were. I came to turn myself in."

"Turn yourself in for what? What are you talking about?" Bob looked at Wilma as if she had morphed into an alien. Or at least grown an extra head.

"For murder. I killed J.D."

"Wilma," Bob fairly roared. "You wouldn't hurt a fly, and we all know it. Don't we, John?"

"Do we?" John retorted. "The way I remember it, if someone confesses, I have to take them into custody and question them. Isn't that the way you heard it, Jenna?"

How unfair. Leave me out of this. I tried to send telepathic messages to John, but he wasn't picking up my signal.

"Isn't that what Bob said yesterday?"

He didn't get to be chief of police by not being persistent, obviously.

"Wilma couldn't have done it." Bob cut John off. "We left the diner and went straight home to watch that 'bad boys' cop show." He turned to look at his wife. "We watch it every Friday night. She was with me the whole night, and I'll swear to that in any court of law you want to take us."

"Is that right, Wilma?" John asked gently.

"Yes. He's right, of course."

"Well, Bob, congratulations. You've given Wilma a good alibi."

"Now, honey, go on home and let me handle things." Bob gave Wilma a peck on the cheek and guided her to the door.

"Just a minute, Bob." John's voice hardened. "You do realize that when you alibied Wilma, you also alibied yourself?"

Bob looked stunned. I guess a night in the slammer had diminished his thought processes.

"Now, why don't you both go on home and leave the police work to me?" He shook his head as he walked out of the office.

Dear Pru,

My boyfriend and I have been dating for three months. I have always known that he smokes dope now and then, but the other day he offered me a joint. I said no, thanks, and he laughed at me. He said I need to learn to live. I said it was more like learn to die. He hasn't called me since. Should I call and apologize?

Who's the Dope?

Dear Who's,

It's not you. Unless you call and apologize. Then there will be two dopes in this equation. What you should do is thank your lucky stars that he quit calling you. Go out and make friends who have fun without depending on substance abuse.

20

It'll all come out in the wash.

Funny how I'd thought it would be perfect if Bob would sell me the athletic club. I'd just never imagined that Lisa would have to be arrested for murder in order to make it happen.

Bob had spent all week trying to get her out of jail, and I'd spent all week trying to get the paperwork through. I felt guilty that I'd succeeded and he hadn't. But however it had happened, the bank called at four and said my money was ready. I had an in with the lawyer, so after I picked up the check, Alex stayed open late for Bob and me to meet at his office. Together we'd transferred ownership.

Five minutes before closing time, I pushed the double doors open and stepped into the Lake View Athletic Club — finally mine.

"Hey, boss, is this a sign of things to

come? Showing up right before we close?" Gail asked jokingly as I walked by where she was gathering her things. "Bob told me. Congratulations."

I nodded. "Thanks." No matter how overbearing and annoying Lisa had acted, it was hard to enjoy the victory knowing she was sitting in a jail cell.

"There are a couple of stragglers. Want me to stay around? Or are you going to lock up?"

"I'll lock up. I'm not staying too long."

Seth and Ricky came by from the showers, gym bags in their hands. "Hey, Jenna. How's it feel to finally own the place?" Seth asked, his cocky grin firmly in place. I hoped he'd gotten over his misplaced affection for me.

"Good. Thanks."

Ricky nodded. "Congrats on your new venture."

"Does this mean you're going to be too busy for all those questions?" Seth asked.

Ricky cleared his throat and looked uncomfortable. "We need to go, man."

"Aw, don't be shy around Jenna. In between her amateur investigating, she's been real curious about you, too."

My face grew hot. Seth and his jealousy. He thought I'd been asking about Ricky because I was interested in him romantically. Amelia was going to kill me. So much for being subtle.

"I —"

Ricky flashed me an easy smile and slapped Seth on his shoulder. "Your jealousy is showing, man. But I'm pretty sure she's taken, and so am I. So let's get going."

Seth followed him out, and I turned to Gail with a grimace. "What is it about men? Once you're attached, they suddenly find you irresistible."

"I wouldn't know," she muttered.

I frowned.

Her face reddened. "Sorry."

"Vini?"

She nodded. "Not that he knows I'm alive. As anything other than a good friend."

"He doesn't know what he's missing." But he would pretty soon if I had anything to say about it.

She gave me a wry grin. "Who needs men? I think I'm going to go get some New York Super Fudge Chunk and drown my miseries in ice cream."

"Good idea. I'm going to go see if the office looks any different now that it's really mine."

In the office, I glared up at the wall. Lisa had once again replaced my beach scenes with modern art pictures. I sighed. At least I knew where to find them this time. She'd done the same thing when I was away in Branson, and I'd had to search the whole place before I finally found them in the janitor's closet next to the pool.

As I jogged down the well-lit but deserted hallway, I slipped my cell phone from my pocket and into my hand. The emptiness of the huge building creeped me out. It was the same way when I was at the newspaper office late at night. So many tiny unexplained noises punctuated the quietness.

When I opened the door to the pool area, shadows from the underwater lights rippled across the surface of the Olympic-size swimming pool. The familiar sound of the pumping system soothed my nerves. Maybe some people would consider that creepy, but my mood lightened, and I slowed to a walk, smiling at the blue octagon of water. This was one place that I didn't need other people around — this was my safe place. Suddenly, the realization that I actually owned the pool surged through me. I fought the urge to run to the locker room, get into my swimsuit, and dive into the deep end. There'd be time for that after I retrieved my pictures.

I unlocked the janitor's closet and pulled

the string to turn on the lone lightbulb. Without wasting any time, I squatted down to look behind the shelves. Sure enough, there were my pictures. Same as before. But never again. Unless I decided to retire them and redecorate. And even then, I wouldn't put them in the chlorine-saturated air of the pool closet, something Lisa had no doubt done on purpose.

Still squatting, I put my cell phone on the floor behind me and gently slid the wooden frames from their hiding place. A manila envelope tumbled out with them. I propped the pictures against the wall and sank down cross-legged in the open doorway. With Lisa's penchant for hiding things here, there was no telling what the envelope contained. And with my penchant for being curious, there was no chance I wouldn't open it.

When I turned the envelope up, two newspaper clippings fluttered into my lap. I caught the first one and held it up to the light. It was from a Memphis newspaper, *The Commercial Appeal.*

Foul Play Suspected in Death of Cop's Wife, blared the headline. I scanned the article. Judy Richardson had been found dead at the bottom of a stairwell in the apartment building where she and her husband, detective Eric Richardson, resided.

Bruises on her shoulders and back indicated that she had possibly been pushed. Although not officially a suspect, Mr. Richardson was listed as a person of interest. Investigation was ongoing.

I squinted at the photo of the young cop. He looked so familiar. My eyes went to the date of the article. Five years ago. I glanced at the photo again. Suddenly, my heart jumped. Even though I'd never heard that name, I knew Eric Richardson.

I didn't know why these clippings were here, but I did know one thing. I'd promised Amelia I'd let her know if I found out anything about her future son-in-law. And that lopsided grin definitely belonged to Ricky Richards.

I reached behind me for my phone; then my hand froze as the second headline caught my eye: LOCAL DETECTIVE EXONERATED IN WIFE'S MURDER. Police detective Eric Richardson had an airtight alibi for the time of his wife's murder. He and a local businessman were fishing at Tunica Lake during the time of the murder. "I will cooperate with the police in every way to find the murderer of my beloved wife, Judy."

I pulled my hand back. What purpose would be served by calling Amelia? He'd been through so much. No wonder he'd changed his name. And if the presence of these clippings was any indication, exonerated or not, his past had followed him to Lake View. Had someone been blackmailing him? Even though he'd been cleared, Amelia probably wouldn't take it very well that he'd been suspected of killing his wife.

I skimmed the rest of the article. Police had been about to arrest Richardson when local businessman J.D. Finley came forward with his alibi. I sucked in my breath. Someone had been blackmailing him all right.

But he'd apparently gotten tired of it.

I reached for my phone again. "How could I have been so stupid?"

A searing pain shot through my hand. I jerked around and tried to get to my feet but stumbled onto my knees. A tall shadow loomed over me, a big black boot firmly planted on my hand.

"Too smart for your own good if you ask me," Ricky snarled. I stared up into the barrel of a gun, complete with silencer. "Asking questions about me was a big mistake."

"My hand," I breathed. He ground his boot like he was stomping a bug. I bit my lip to keep from giving him the satisfaction of hearing me cry out, but I couldn't hold back a whimper. Hot tears spilled onto my cheeks.

"Stand up nice and slow," he ordered, all trace of "good ol' boy" gone from his voice.

I cradled my hand against my stomach and pushed to my feet.

"If you'd have kept your nose out of things, this would have all been over."

"Is that what your wife did?" I asked, blinking the tears away. "Asked too many questions?"

He jerked my arm, and I winced. "Judy's death was an accident! I lost my temper and pushed her. I didn't mean for her to die."

"Was J.D.'s death an accident, too?" I croaked out.

He laughed, and my blood ran cold. "I planned J.D.'s killing down to the last detail."

"So he was blackmailing you?"

"J.D. did a job and got paid. But he made the mistake of thinking he held all the cards when he found me again. At first I went along with him. I paid him what I had left of Judy's insurance money, but he got greedy."

He shoved the gun barrel into my ribs. "Too bad Bob's no-good daughter is in jail. I could set her up for killing you, too. Guess you'll have to have an unfortunate accident instead. I'm sure she hid some of your stuff up in the attic, and that staircase is so narrow. . . ." He nudged me forward.

I dragged my feet, my brain racing. If I struggled, he'd shoot me, but as we neared the pool, a memory flashed into my mind. Seth had said Ricky told him, "If God intended us to swim, he'd have given us fins."

We walked by the ten-foot marker, and I stumbled. He instinctively reached toward me. I slammed my body hard into his, grateful to see the gun go spiraling through the air just before we hit the water. A second later, my bright idea didn't seem so bright. He couldn't swim, but he had a death grip on me. Literally.

In every lifesaving class I'd ever taken, we'd learned how to keep someone from drowning you while you were trying to save them. But we'd learned nothing about how to let them drown and save yourself. Not that I wanted him to drown. I just needed him unconscious. Right now our futures were joined and looking pretty dismal. He pulled my head under again.

Suddenly, I felt and heard another splash. As my lungs burned for air, I groaned inside. Had he brought an ally with him? A lookout who'd come to rescue him and finish me off? I struggled to the surface and saw that the third person in the water was

Seth, who did indeed seem to be trying to rescue Ricky. Panicked, Ricky continued to claw and fight. Seth drew back his fist and clipped Ricky on the jaw.

Ricky's grip on me immediately relaxed, and I scrambled away from the men and over to the ladder. I climbed out of the water and was debating running when I spotted the gun at my feet. Just as Seth came out of the water dragging Ricky, I snatched it up and pointed it toward the two men.

Seth's eyes grew wide. "Jenna Stafford, have you lost your mind? I had no choice but to knock him out. He was drowning me. And you, too, for that matter."

My slippery grip wavered, but I forced myself to hold steady. "Put him down."

He obeyed me and backed up a step with his hands up. "What did I do?"

"What are you doing here?"

He dropped his gaze to the floor. "Uh. I saw Ricky's car in the parking lot and yours. And I . . . I . . . Doggone it, Jenna. I wanted to see if my partner had gone after the girl he knew I —" He dropped his hands. "I wasn't breaking in or anything. And what about you? Why did you two decide to go for a swim with your clothes on?"

Ricky groaned, and I trained the gun on

him. I could see the truth all over Seth's face. All Seth was guilty of was jealousy. Ricky was definitely in it alone. "It's a long story." I motioned with the gun toward the newspaper clippings still lying on the floor in the closet doorway.

With a wary look at me, Seth walked over and picked them up. I kept one eye on the still unconscious Ricky as I watched Seth read the articles. A gamut of emotions flitted across his face. When he finished, his cheeks were red with anger. "He's the killer?"

I nodded. He picked up his cell phone from the side of the pool and called for backup. Within minutes, sirens wailed through the quiet night.

"Jenna!" Carly waved a paper at me as she and Elliott walked up to the basketball court. "I meant to tell you, this came to the diner yesterday." She handed me a postcard.

I looked down at the picture, a cartoon of a red mustang and a leggy blond.

"I don't believe it." I grinned. "Listen to this. 'Hey, chickie, I finally planted my roots practically in my granny's backyard. And the next-door neighbor is a really nice fellow. A preacher, no less. Did I mention he's single? Wink, wink. Thanks for hanging with me when I was in need of a pal. Jolene.' "

"A preacher?" Carly shook her head. "That man won't know what hit him."

Zac dribbled his basketball up to us. "Y'all ready to choose teams? I got Elliott."

Elliott held out his hands, and Zac threw him the ball. He passed it to Alex, who made a jump shot.

When they were gone, Carly turned back to me. "Alice called yesterday. She and Harvey are settling down in Florida. She told me they'd found a little diner for sale, so she keeps having to remind Harvey what the word *retired* means."

I smiled. "Sounds like they're happy. Bob came to the club yesterday. First time he's been there since we signed the papers three weeks ago. He didn't come right out and say it, but he hinted that Lisa's in a twelve-step program for her gambling problem. He said something like, 'It'll take a lot of work, but Lisa's got a good man behind her,' so I assume she and Larry are working things out. Oh, I almost forgot. He also said that Lisa had asked J.D. to take my pictures to the pool closet. Apparently he decided to stash his blackmail stuff there, as well."

"Well, look who's here." Alex walked over from the court to stand beside me as Seth sauntered toward us. He relaxed slightly as

Tiffany emerged from the other side of the truck and jogged in Seth's wake. "Hey, y'all, ready to play?"

Tiffany appeared to have lost weight since Ricky's arrest, but she wore a smile along with her fitted jeans and cute T-shirt. Her hair was pulled into a casual ponytail, but she looked good. And happy.

Seth stepped back to let her go first, and I suddenly remembered him being so defensive with me when he thought I was trying to steal Tiffany's man. What had he said? That she was a "real sweet girl"? Tiffany might get her happy ending after all.

"Hey, Seth. John too scared of gettin' whupped to show up?" Alex asked.

"Oh, didn't you hear? Denise went into labor right after Sunday school."

Carly glanced at me. "Do you think we should go over to the hospital and check on her?"

Seth shrugged. "You can if you want to, but she had the baby about an hour ago, and everything's fine."

"Wow. That was fast," I said.

"Yeah. It's a girl." Tiffany winked at me. "John said that since she was so curious and impatient, he and Denise were thinking of changing their mind about what to name her."

Alex grinned and put his arm around my shoulders. "Let me guess . . ."

Seth nodded. "Yep, but then they decided Lake View only had room for one Jenna."

We all laughed, and Seth and Tiffany walked on over to the basketball court.

Alex pulled me close and brushed a stray curl back from my face. "I sure am glad Lake View has you. I can't imagine our lives if we hadn't found each other again."

I stared into his blue eyes, and in that moment my whole life seemed to click into place, as if I were seeing the big picture for the very first time. Alex's mother's words echoed in my head. All the disappointments and trials in my life — not winning the Olympics, losing a student, and even not buying the health club right away — had just been part of my path. But God had taken that path and used it to bring me to where I stood today. In Alex's arms.

I couldn't have asked for anything more.

ABOUT THE AUTHORS

Sisters **Christine Pearle Lynxwiler, Jan Pearle Reynolds,** and **Sandy Pearle Gaskin** are usually on the same page. And it's most often a page from their favorite mystery. So when the idea for a Christian cozy mystery series came up during Sunday dinner at Mama's, they became determined to take their dream further than just table talk. Thus, the Sleuthing Sisters mystery series was born.

Christine writes full-time. She and her husband, Kevin, live with their two children in the beautiful Ozark Mountains and enjoy kayaking on the nearby Spring River. **Jan,** part-time writer and full-time office manager, and her husband, Steve, love to spend time with their two adult children and their granddogs on the lake or just relaxing at home. **Sandy,** part-time writer and retired teacher, works with her husband, Bart, managing their manufacturing business.

With their daughter off to college, she hopes to devote more time to writing. The three sisters love to hear from readers by e-mail at sleuthingsisters@yahoo.com.

You may correspond with these authors by writing:

Christine Lynxwiler, Sandy Gaskin,
  Jan Reynolds
Author Relations
PO Box 721
Uhrichsville, OH 44683